Dear Reader,

It is an honor to bring you one of my stories this month because Harlequin American Romance is celebrating its 20th anniversary. Writing for this line has been such a wonderful experience. Our books are heartwarming, happy stories. I feel good when I finish writing one, and I hope you feel as good when you finish reading one.

Heart, Home & Happiness... Those three words describe Harlequin American Romance stories best. Each time I write a new one, I'll imagine you with a special smile on your face as you read it.

This book is also special because it is my 50th title for Harlequin and Silhouette Books. Over the years my editors have been very supportive, making the creative process—from idea to published book—an enjoyable one. Needless to say, I'm glad that they like cowboys, since they are my favorite hero types. Here's to another fifty stories!

Best wishes!

Judy Christenberry

Dear Reader,

Our yearlong twentieth-anniversary celebration continues with a spectacular lineup, starting with *Saved by a Texas-Sized Wedding*, beloved author Judy Christenberry's 50th book. Don't miss this delightful addition to the popular series TOTS FOR TEXANS. It's a marriage-of-convenience story that will warm your heart!

Priceless Marriage by Bonnie Gardner is the latest installment in the MILLIONAIRE, MONTANA continuity series, in which a "Main Street Millionaire" claims her "ex" as her own. Jacqueline Diamond pens another charming story in THE BABIES OF DOCTORS CIRCLE series with *Prescription: Marry Her Immediately*. Here a confirmed bachelor doctor enlists the help of his gorgeous best friend in order to win custody of his orphaned niece and nephew. And let us welcome a new author to the Harlequin American Romance family. Kaitlyn Rice makes her sparkling debut with *Ten Acres and Twins*.

It's an exciting year for Harlequin American Romance, and we invite you to join the celebration this month and far into the future!

Melissa Jeglinski
Associate Senior Editor
Harlequin American Romance

Judy Christenberry

SAVED BY A TEXAS-SIZED WEDDING

HARLEQUIN®

TORONTO • NEW YORK • LONDON
AMSTERDAM • PARIS • SYDNEY • HAMBURG
STOCKHOLM • ATHENS • TOKYO • MILAN • MADRID
PRAGUE • WARSAW • BUDAPEST • AUCKLAND

ISBN 0-373-16969-8

SAVED BY A TEXAS-SIZED WEDDING

Copyright © 2003 by Judy Russell Christenberry.

ABOUT THE AUTHOR

Judy Christenberry has been writing romances for fifteen years because she loves happy endings as much as her readers do. A former French teacher, Judy now devotes herself to writing full-time. She hopes readers have as much fun reading her stories as she does writing them. She spends her spare time reading, watching her favorite sports teams and keeping track of her two daughters. Judy is a native Texan.

Books by Judy Christenberry

HARLEQUIN AMERICAN ROMANCE

555—FINDING DADDY
579—WHO'S THE DADDY?
612—WANTED: CHRISTMAS
    MOMMY
626—DADDY ON DEMAND
649—COWBOY CUPID*
653—COWBOY DADDY*
661—COWBOY GROOM*
665—COWBOY SURRENDER*
701—IN PAPA BEAR'S BED
726—A COWBOY AT HEART
735—MY DADDY THE DUKE
744—COWBOY COME HOME*
755—COWBOY SANTA
773—ONE HOT DADDY-TO-BE?†
777—SURPRISE—YOU'RE A
    DADDY!†
781—DADDY UNKNOWN†
785—THE LAST STUBBORN COWBOY†
802—BABY 2000

817—THE GREAT TEXAS WEDDING
    BARGAIN†
842—THE $10,000,000 TEXAS
    WEDDING†
853—PATCHWORK FAMILY
867—RENT A MILLIONAIRE GROOM
878—STRUCK BY THE TEXAS
    MATCHMAKERS†
885—RANDALL PRIDE*
901—TRIPLET SECRET BABIES
918—RANDALL RICHES*
930—RANDALL HONOR*
950—RANDALL WEDDING*
969—SAVED BY A TEXAS-SIZED
    WEDDING†

*Brides for Brothers
†Tots for Texans

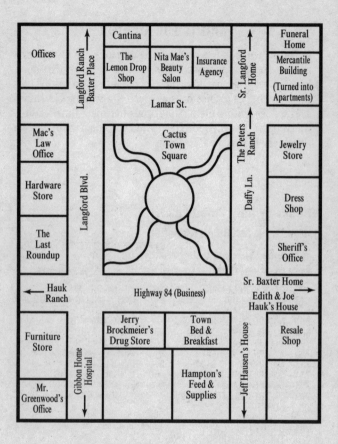

Prologue

Suzanne McCoy stepped out on the front porch, closing the door behind her, and drew a deep breath. The air was quite different than the air in Dallas, where she'd lived until six days ago. That was when her life had drastically changed. Her cousin Mary Lee and her husband had been killed in a car accident; an elderly man had had a heart attack at the wheel of his truck and crashed into them.

Mary Lee and Rodger had moved to Cactus, a small town in west Texas, a year ago. Suzanne had missed them so much. Josh, now four, had been three years old. And Mandy had only been one, just walking and talking. She'd changed so much in a year.

Suzanne leaned against the railing on the porch. Mary Lee had left the children to her to raise. It hadn't taken much time for Suzanne to decide to give up her life in Dallas and come here. Pushing papers at an insurance company didn't seem important compared to helping Josh and Mandy deal with their loss and helping them grow up. She'd always wanted children, but she hadn't been nearly as interested in marriage. That involved men, and every man in her life from her father on had betrayed her.

Since everything seemed peaceful inside the house where the children were sleeping, Suzanne moved off the porch to walk slowly toward the bunkhouse. Until today, she'd scarcely had time to think about, much less do anything about, their situation, other than care for the children. Now she had a couple of questions. She figured the best person to answer them would be the manager Rodger had hired.

A soft breeze blew this evening, sending a shiver or two up her spine. As she got closer to the bunkhouse, the peace went away, too. She could hear voices. There was even laughing. She hadn't laughed since she'd gotten the news about Mary Lee and Rodger. She paused outside the door, not wanting to interrupt. She heard someone banging on something, as if calling everyone to order. She relaxed, until she heard a man declare, "We're all going to be rich! We've made a good start. And we'll get more 'cause the boss lady don't know nothing about ranchin'. She's too busy with those kids."

Suzanne froze. Then liquid heat bubbled through her, past any logical thought or careful planning. She threw back the door and stomped into the room, marched up to the man at the head of the group and slugged him as hard as she could. Then she looked at the rest of them. "This boss lady catches on fast. You've got fifteen minutes to clear out. The sheriff will be here by then and I'll be pressing charges!''

Pandemonium reigned. As her anger receded to a more manageable level, she realized it would've been better to creep away and call the sheriff first. But it was too late for that now.

When the dust settled, only an old man sat in the corner of the room, whittling on a piece of wood.

''Aren't you scared about the sheriff's arrival?'' she asked with disdain.

''Nope. Haven't done anything wrong. I've been working here since I was fifteen. I didn't rob you, ma'am. I told them I'd have nothing to do with those shenanigans.''

''Why didn't you warn me?''

''I was thinking about it. They didn't get away with too much. You've still got a herd left. Just won't have as much profit as you might've had. But you've got a real problem.''

''What?''

''Who's gonna do the work?''

''Better that I do it than to let them get away with robbing those two children blind!''

''Yes, ma'am. But I don't think you know anything about cattle…or ranching.'' He turned and spit tobacco juice to the side. Since there were already a few stains on the floor, she didn't stop him. Besides, she was beginning to realize he was right. She had a real problem.

''How many cowboys do I need to run this place?''

''Well now, if they were trained like Ryan's men,

you could manage with four or five. But his men are a mite above average.''

"Who is Ryan?"

"Ryan Walker. Neighbor to the west."

"Then I probably met him at the funeral."

"Mebbe. He knows ranching better'n anyone."

"Do you think he'll loan me some help?"

"Nope. He has a big place."

Suzanne sighed in frustration. "Then what am I going to do?"

"Go talk to the sheriff, first thing in the morning."

Chapter One

"Come along, Josh," Suzanne said, looking down at the boy. Though he held her hand, he was pulling back every step of the way.

The door opened and a big man came through it, obviously in a hurry. He grabbed her shoulders to stop from knocking her down.

"Sorry, ma'am. I didn't see you."

Before she could pull herself together, he tipped his hat and was gone.

"Well! He was certainly in a hurry." She tightened her grip on Mandy. "Are you all right, sweetheart?"

The child nodded her head and then hid it in Suzanne's red-brown hair.

"How about you, Josh? He didn't step on you, did he?"

"No, Susie."

With a sigh, she stepped into the office. "I need to see Sheriff Cal Baxter, if he's in."

"Sure he's in. Those Mary Lee and Rodger's

children? Poor babies. Who shall I tell him is calling?''

''Suzanne McCoy, guardian to Josh and Mandy.''

''Well, now, you just have a seat. My name's Gladys. I'll be right back.''

With a sigh, Suzanne took one of the chairs. She released Josh's hand and patted the chair next to her. ''Sit down, honey. I know you're still sleepy.''

The little boy slumped against the chair. He hadn't smiled once since Suzanne had gotten to Cactus. She was worried about him. Mandy had cried for her mother every morning so far, though she forgot her tears quickly. But when she slipped and called Suzanne Mama, Josh reminded Mandy that her name was Susie. That's what Mary Lee used to call her.

Gladys reappeared with another tall cowboy behind her.

''Morning, Miss McCoy. Come on in the office. Do you want Gladys to look after the little ones?''

''No, they'd better come with me.''

When they were settled in the chairs before the sheriff's desk, she explained about the thieving that had been going on and what she'd done about it. ''I realized in the middle of confronting them that they might not react well, so I told them I'd already called you. I know I should've told you first and followed your directions. I lost my temper,'' she added, her voice dropping.

He smiled. ''You're not the only one with a temper in Cactus. One of your neighbors just came in to tell me he thought something was going on. I was going to come see you.''

''Oh, that's nice of him.''

''Yeah.''

''The old man said he was *thinking* about telling me,'' she said in disgust.

''I reckon you mean old Al.''

''Yes, I think his name was Al.''

''Well, you'll have to forgive old Al. He's in his eighties and that's been his only home. He doesn't move too fast these days.''

''I see. But he pointed out that I'd need some hands to run the ranch. I—I don't know anything about ranching.''

''Best you talk with Ryan Walker. He's your neighbor who just came in to warn me. He knows the most about ranching around here. And being next door will be convenient. Or you can visit the farm agent, but he's…new on the job. He may not be able to offer much.''

''And you'll catch those cowhands?''

''I'll keep my eye out for them, me and my deputies, but I imagine they've left the state. I'll talk to Al about what they did.''

''Thank you, sheriff.''

Once she and the kids were outside, standing on the sidewalk, she debated her next option. She found the farm agent's office and noted that it didn't open until eight. Then she spotted The Lemon Drop Shop across the town square. A quick look at Josh made her decision. ''Josh, let's go have a lemonade and a cookie or something while we wait to see the farm agent. Okay?''

The boy perked up a little, but not much. He shrugged, though he followed her a little less reluctantly. When they got inside, she found they were serving sausage rolls and sweet rolls. She made the choices for all three of them and moved to the cash register to pay.

"Hello. You're the guardian of Mary Lee and Rodger's children, aren't you?"

Suzanne looked up in surprise. "Yes, I am. I'm sorry, I don't—"

"No, of course you don't. I'm Katherine Dawson. Most people call me Katie. Why don't you pick a table and I'll bring over your order."

"Oh, that would be so nice of you." Suzanne relaxed a little. She stepped outside and chose an empty table. Josh crawled up into a chair and she sat Mandy down in the one next to him. Then she took the third seat. Katie appeared with a large tray holding their lemonades and the rolls she'd ordered.

"Mind if I sit with you a few minutes?" Katie asked.

Suzanne shook her head no and introduced herself. "I've moved from Dallas to take care of the children."

"Oh, good. You're going to stay. We were afraid you'd take the children back to Dallas."

Suzanne shook her head, then added, "Maybe I should. I don't know anything about ranching and—" she paused and then explained what had happened the previous night.

"Oh, no, how awful for you."

"What's wrong, Katie?" asked an older woman standing with a friend behind their table.

"Oh, good morning, Mabel, Florence. Have you met Suzanne McCoy?" She looked at Suzanne. "Do you mind if these two ladies join us?"

"No, of course not," Suzanne automatically agreed, though she wasn't sure she wanted to tell her story to everyone.

It was Katie, however, who told her friends what had happened. Then she turned to Suzanne. "What are you going to do?"

"Well, the sheriff—"

"He's my son," Mabel Baxter inserted proudly.

"Oh, well, he said he would look for the trouble-makers, but he doubted any of them would hang around."

"So?" Florence asked.

"I've got to find someone who knows about ranching, some cowboys to take care of what herd we have left."

"See Ryan Walker," Mabel said with a determined nod of her chin.

"That's what your son said."

"He's right. Ryan is a great rancher," Florence agreed. Then she looked as if an idea had struck her. She looked at Mabel, then Suzanne. "Tell me, dear, are you—involved with anyone?"

Suzanne stared at her blankly. The sudden switch of subject surprised her. Finally she said, "No. I don't know anyone here."

"So you didn't leave any broken hearts in Dallas?"

"No. But about my ranch—"

"Yes. I was thinking, you see, Ryan needs a baby-sitter," Florence said, again surprising Suzanne.

"He does?"

"Yes. Beth is—how old is Beth, Katie?"

"She just turned three. Her mother didn't like the ranching life and ran away with a city man. Ryan has raised Beth by himself since she was six months old. Only now she's getting too big for him to take her everywhere he goes."

"And you think if I offered to baby-sit Beth he'd help me?" Suzanne asked skeptically.

"It would be better if you married him," Mabel said clearly.

Suzanne stared at her as if she were crazy.

Katie hurriedly said, "Mabel is teasing you. But you should talk to Ryan. You also have a good water supply on your place. Ryan might make a deal for some split water rights."

Suzanne nodded and dropped the subject, urging the children to eat their rolls so they could visit the farm agent. When she left the shop, she saw the two older women hurrying off in another direction.

The farm agent was no help at all, except to suggest she talk to Ryan Walker. She thanked him and took the kids home.

The rest of the day, she thought about the suggestions she'd received in town. She drafted Al to baby-sit when the sun went down. He told her Ryan wouldn't come home until then. It occurred to her that the man who'd almost knocked her down might be Ryan Walker. If he was, he was a very intimidating man.

As the sun set, she checked her appearance in the mirror. She'd put on one of her business suits, hoping to impress him with her professionalism. She'd pulled her long red-brown hair back to a knot on her neck. She wanted to look cool and calm. Okay, she was ready to face the best rancher in the county.

With a deep breath, she made sure Al was happy with the kids. She'd made popcorn and poured some soda for them. She thought things went better when they had something to eat. "I'll be back as soon as I can," she said, faking cheeriness.

"Are you sure?" Josh asked, frowning.

"I'm just going to our neighbor's house, Josh. I won't stay long." Their parents had just gone out for a little while and they'd never come back. Josh didn't trust her promise.

He nodded and looked the other way. Suzanne thought she saw tears in his eyes, but Al waved her off and asked Josh to change the channel on the television. Having something to do helped Josh. Amazing that Al understood that.

She carefully drove in the direction Al had shown her. He said it was the next ranch, just a little ways down the road. She kept looking for a house, or at least a driveway. After twenty minutes, she wondered if she'd gone in the wrong direction. Then she saw a house. The mailbox on the side of the road said Walker, so she guessed she'd finally found the infamous Ryan Walker. She pulled up to the porch and got out of her car.

She dusted off her black suit and climbed the steps to the porch. She couldn't see any lights on in the house, but maybe the kitchen and den were in the back of the house and couldn't be seen from the road. She knocked, but there was no response. She knocked again, louder this time. The third time she pounded.

She wasn't going away without talking to the man. She climbed down the steps and walked around to the back of the house. There were no lights visible back there either. She returned to the front porch and sat down on the top step, wondering what she should do.

Then she saw lights coming down the road. Maybe he'd run into town for a few minutes and was now returning. She hoped so.

She stood, tucking a strand of hair into place as a black truck pulled in, passing her car and continuing on past the house. She walked to the side of the house to see if it stopped in the back. When it did, she drew a deep sigh of relief.

RYAN WALKER was tired. He'd spent a long day in the saddle. Then he'd gone into town to pick up Beth, his three-year-old daughter from his cousin Millie. He didn't want company, especially company dressed like a city woman. In fact, when he'd first seen the woman on his porch, he'd been afraid it was Tiffany, his ex-wife. He sure didn't want to see her ever again.

He had things to do that night. Especially after what Millie had told him. The first thing he needed to do was to talk to Mabel and Florence and make it clear he wasn't interested in getting married. Millie told him they had visited her, telling her she'd be doing him a favor if she stopped taking care of Beth. Then he'd marry the new lady in town. Fool women!

"Daddy? What's the matter?" Beth asked, staring at him.

"I'm too tired for company, sugar. There's a lady at our front door."

"Why?"

He thought of several answers, but Beth was only three. He didn't want to upset his beloved daughter.

"I don't know. I'll find out while you wash your hands for dinner."

"Are we going to eat those hamburgers?"

"We sure are." He'd driven through a fast-food place after he'd picked up Beth. He was too tired to cook tonight.

He parked the truck and took his daughter into the house. "Go wash up. I'll be right back."

Then he walked through the house to the front door, seldom opened because his friends always came to the back door. He clicked on the porch light as he spoke. "Hello."

"Oh! Mr. Walker. You are Mr. Walker, aren't you?"

Damn it! The woman was the one he'd almost run down this morning. Her vibrant red hair was all tied up tonight, but he'd noticed it this morning. She was dressed in city clothes.

"Yeah. What do you want?" He knew his voice was gruff, not inviting, but he didn't believe in spending much time around beautiful city women. They didn't fit into his world.

"I understand you're the authority on ranching in the county." Her voice was cool, skepticism in it, which he resented.

"Yeah, probably."

"I'm your neighbor to the east. My name is Suzanne McCoy. I'm guardian to Mary Lee and Rodger Howe's children." She waited, as if she expected him to say something, but he only nodded. "I have a problem."

"What?"

"I don't have any employees except for old Al."

"What happened to them?"

"I fired them because they were stealing from the children." She held her chin up as if she expected him to tell her she'd made a mistake.

"Good. I wasn't sure you knew."

She looked down. "I didn't until last night when I heard them bragging. And I fired them before I called the sheriff. They quickly left the ranch, and now no one knows where they are."

"And?"

"I need some cowboys, Mr. Walker. And I know nothing about what they do or how I can tell if they're good, honest men. Everyone I talked to in town told me to speak to you. Please, will you help me?"

"Did you talk to Florence and Mabel?"

"Well, yes, I did."

"Well, Miss McCoy, I'll loan you a couple of hands for a week. That's the most I can spare. But no matter what Mabel and Florence said, I'm not going to marry you, no matter what you say!"

Chapter Two

Suzanne took a step back, her mouth gaping open. Was the man crazy? "What?"

"You heard me. Those women are always trying to match people up, but I'm not that desperate!"

Her cheeks flamed and her temper boiled. "Neither am I!" she snapped.

"Why do you look so surprised? Didn't they suggest it?"

She started to say that no one in their right mind would suggest such a thing, but then she remembered Mabel's comment. "Mabel mentioned something about marriage, but I assumed she was joking."

"Well, now you know she wasn't. And I'm not interested. Okay? Doug and Hinney will be over in the morning." He started to close the door and Suzanne stopped him.

"What Mabel and Florence suggested was that we barter."

"Barter? I don't think you have anything I want."

His words were insulting, and she almost gave up.

But she needed help. Clenching her teeth, she muttered one word. "Baby-sitting."

"Daddy?" Beth asked as she pushed past his legs to stand in front of him, looking at the woman.

"Beth, go back to the kitchen. You can go ahead and start eating, okay?"

Suzanne noted that his voice gentled when he spoke to his child. She squatted down. "Hello, Beth. My name is Suzanne. How are you?"

"Fine," Beth said with a big smile.

"Beth, go to the kitchen at once!" This time his voice wasn't gentle. It was harsh and threatening. His daughter looked at him in surprise and then scurried back down the long hall.

"I wasn't going to hurt her," she protested.

"You don't know anything about her, and I'd like to keep it that way. Even for baby-sitting, I'm not going to take over your ranch. That's what you wanted, wasn't it?"

She drew herself up straight, throwing back her shoulders. "They also mentioned water rights." She waited for his reaction.

"Yeah. You've got good water and I don't. Congratulations. My two men will be there in the morning. Figure out something before the week is up." Then he closed the door in her face.

Suzanne was furious at his rudeness. But she didn't dare bang on the door again. He might cancel the two men coming over tomorrow for a week. They were better than nothing. Maybe with Al to help them, they could take care of things for a week. Surely by then she'd find some cowboys who were looking for work. She had to. One way or another she would preserve Josh and Mandy's heritage.

SUZANNE WAS UP before daylight the next morning, wanting to greet the two cowboys Ryan Walker had said he would send over. She'd told Al the night before of Ryan Walker's offer of temporary help.

"I'm going to do the cooking today for the three of you. I'd like you to do what you can to help them." She knew such work would be hard on the old man, but he readily agreed.

Just as the sun first peeped over the skyline in the east, she heard a truck pull in to their place. She looked out the window and saw the horse trailer behind it. This had to be Doug and "Hinney." What an odd name.

She hurried out and welcomed them. "Have you had breakfast? I can cook something quickly."

"Yes, ma'am, we had breakfast."

"All right. I'll have lunch ready at one."

They both seemed embarrassed, but she gave them a bright smile and went back inside. She wanted Mr. Know-It-All Walker to know that she could provide for the men as well as he could. She spent the morning baking a cake for lunch, mixing up a special beef casserole, and calling every person she could think of who might be able to help her find some cowboys.

Unfortunately, she heard the same thing over and over again. "Call Ryan Walker. He'd know if there are any good ones available."

After the fifth such response, she quit trying.

She'd had the children coloring some pictures at the kitchen table while she worked, but she wanted them to eat before the men came in. She had them clear the table and go wash their hands.

Once they had eaten their lunch, she put Mandy down for her nap and reminded Josh that it was quiet time. He was supposed to remain in his room, preferably on his bed, reading or looking at picture books.

Then she cleared the table and set it again for the three men. Even though it was early spring, it was warm outside during the day, so she had tall glasses of sweetened tea, ice cubes floating in them, waiting for the workmen.

"Wow, Miz McCoy, this looks good," Doug told her as they came in.

She took the casserole out of the oven and the salad out of the refrigerator. She also had a bowl of corn, because she'd been told by her cousin that hearty food was important for hard-working cowboys. Hot rolls completed the lunch menu. When she served them big chunks of chocolate cake after they'd finished off the casserole, they groaned with pleasure.

"I just want you to know I appreciate your work."

"Yes, ma'am," they agreed enthusiastically.

She repeated the process that night for dinner.

"But, ma'am, we're expected at the supper table over at Ryan's," Hinney protested.

"As hard as you've worked, you probably deserve two dinners. Besides, I've got too much cake left over.''

The men fell into their chairs.

Suzanne felt a surge of triumph, knowing Ryan Walker would know she'd treated his men well.

RYAN WORRIED all day about his two men working on the Howe place. The new owner, Rodger Howe, hadn't been a bad man. Just unknowledgeable. He'd visited Ryan several times to ask for advice. Ryan hadn't minded. That was how a man learned. The fact that he'd learned at his grandfather's and father's knees from the time he was old enough to walk made him grateful and willing to share his knowledge.

But not with a city lady. He hoped she fed his men. She probably had only served them salads. That seemed to be the only thing city women knew to fix. He left word for the men to check in with him after they got back.

He ran into town to pick up Beth. He'd told his cousin he'd have someone to take care of Beth by the end of the week. He didn't want her to lose a job opportunity that would pay her more money than he was paying her. Millie had used the excuse of her baby-sitting options to urge him to consider Florence and Mabel's marriage suggestion.

All the way home he worried about how he was going to find someone to take care of Beth. When she started school, most of her day would be covered. Except for holidays and summer vacations. Damn. He might as well figure on a permanent housekeeper. A nice meal ready in the evenings would be a bonus. He occasionally even took Beth to the bunkhouse to eat. But, though they tried, the men would forget themselves and let loose an inappropriate word. Beth was old enough to notice now.

He fed her fast food again tonight while he waited for the men to report. Finally he called the bunkhouse. His manager answered.

"Steve, haven't the guys gotten back yet?"

"Just got in, boss. I'll send them right up."

He tucked Beth into bed and stepped out on the back porch to wait for the men.

"Howdy, boss," Doug said cheerfully. "Everything went fine today, though it's sad that those men did so little work and then stole from them kids."

"Hinney, you okay, too?"

"Yeah, boss, she's a good cook. And she didn't make fun of my name."

"Good," Ryan said, trying not to grind his teeth. "You can tell her you have to come home for lunch if you want."

Both men jumped to their feet and yelled no, then suddenly sat back down, embarrassed by their reactions.

Ryan eyed them carefully. "She cooks that good, does she?"

Surprisingly, it was shy Hinney who answered. "Yeah, and she makes it all pretty. And she's so pretty!" he added, his cheeks turning red.

Ryan definitely ground his teeth. "Tell me about

the work,'' he ordered sharply, unwilling to listen to any more praise about Ms. Suzanne McCoy.

When they finished their report, Ryan, though he already knew the answer, asked if they'd mind going again the next day. He got the answer he expected, a resounding agreement. He discussed with them what they would do the next day. Then he sent them off to the bunkhouse.

He stayed on the porch, his feelings torn. He hated to see the land and animals mistreated as they had been by that thieving crew. He was pleased his men were helping. But he wanted to keep his distance from a city woman…who could cook. Mercy, his men were eating better than he was!

He thought about her offer to baby-sit and share water in return for his help. If she weren't so pretty, he might even consider it, but he was afraid he'd be easily caught by her beauty and then have his heart broken if he did any such thing.

Not that his wife had broken his heart. By the time she'd run away, he'd already realized his mistake. She hadn't contributed much to his life except whining and complaining. And Beth. He was grateful she hadn't taken Beth away with her.

But he wasn't going to make the same mistake twice. He thought about Ms. McCoy last night, in her black suit, her hair tortured into some kind of a knot. She didn't belong here and she wouldn't stay. So much for her.

He just had to wait for her to go back to the city and put the place up for sale. He'd buy it and increase his own place, with good water rights. He looked forward to the day.

SUZANNE ACTUALLY enjoyed the week. She enjoyed the domestic routine and the time spent with Josh and Mandy. She'd found a store in Cactus that carried educational materials and she'd bought several books for the children. Mandy loved to draw, and she was learning her colors. They were going to work on the alphabet next. And Josh was learning words, spelling them and sounding them out.

She loved cooking, especially for an appreciative audience, and the cowboys were definitely that. She'd tried several new recipes with great success. Cooking for hungry men was very rewarding.

She was also keeping the house clean and working on a budget she could submit to the lawyer who held the children's finances. In fact, she was feeling very successful in her new life, except for one thing.

She hadn't found any new employees. Not even one.

She occasionally wondered if Ryan Walker had told the neighbors not to help her. But they offered good advice, lots of sympathy and the ladies even brought desserts over.

Finally, on Thursday evening, she again made the trek to Ryan Walker's ranch house. Again she dressed in a business suit, red this time. It was a power color, especially when combined with her red hair and brown eyes. She put on makeup for the first time since she'd last visited the Walker ranch. She bribed Al to stay with the children and headed west down the county road.

"Go west young man," she muttered an old saying. "Why can't some of Walker's well-trained cowboys come east? I'd love to have Doug and Hinney working for me."

She'd even considered offering them a bonus if they'd leave Ryan Walker, but she refused to stoop to that level. It *was* tempting.

She pulled into the driveway, noting the lack of lights, but she checked to discover the truck he drove was parked around back. She got out of her car and climbed the steps to the porch, knocking on the front door.

She thought there wasn't going to be an answer, but the door slowly opened. She had to look down to find who'd opened it. "Beth!"

"Hi," the little girl said, smiling at her.

Suzanne thought she was adorable, but as a responsible parent now herself, she knew it was dangerous to let children of this age answer the door. "Um, does your daddy know you answered the door?"

Beth shook her head no.

"Is he here?"

"He's on the back porch, talking to Doug and Hinney," Beth said.

That information caught Suzanne by surprise. Did the men report in each evening? That hadn't occurred to her. "Well, why don't you close the door and go back to bed, and I'll walk around to the back porch, okay?"

"Okay," Beth said and slammed the door shut. Suzanne heard little feet padding down the hall.

With a smile on her lips, she walked around the house, regretting wearing her high heels. When she got close she heard male voices talking, but she didn't stop. She wasn't going to listen in on a private conversation again. The last time, though enlightening, had led to a disaster.

Rounding the house, she came to a halt. "Mr. Walker?"

The three men on the porch had been casually sprawled in some chairs and they almost toppled over.

Ryan Walker immediately stood. "Ms. McCoy." His stiff greeting obviously surprised the other two men.

"I'm sorry if I'm interrupting, but I need to talk to you."

"How did you know I was back here?" he asked, his voice gruff, as if he were accusing her of sneaking around.

She looked him straight in the eye. "Beth told me when she answered the door." She paused, then couldn't resist adding, "I don't consider that safe behavior for a child that young."

The moment she'd said Beth's name, his head had snapped around to the back door. "I'll be right back," he growled and stomped into the house.

"Hi, guys. You haven't gotten in trouble for working for me, have you?"

"No, Miss Suzanne," Doug said, grinning. "Boss

might fire us if we keep putting on weight, though. Your cooking is so good, we're getting fat.''

"Nonsense, you haven't gained weight," Suzanne assured them with a warm smile.

A stern voice said, ''Flattery won't persuade them to go to work for you, if that's what you're after.'' Walker moved from out of the shadows to glare at her.

''I know,'' she agreed, keeping her composure.

''But chocolate cake might,'' Hinney said softly. Both cowhands laughed and Suzanne smiled, but Walker continued to glare.

The cowhands recognized danger when they saw it. ''Uh, reckon we'll go on to bed, boss, if we're finished.'' The two of them headed for the bunkhouse without waiting for their boss's response.

''They were just teasing,'' she said calmly, wishing that would be all it took to get a good staff. ''I need to talk to you, Mr. Walker.''

With narrowed eyes, he waved to one of the chairs the cowboys had used. ''Have a seat, Ms. McCoy.''

She did as he asked, but she was uncomfortable, and she didn't think he was happy either. ''You told me to have my problem solved by the end of the week.'' She paused, but he didn't say anything. ''I haven't found even one employee, Mr. Walker, and I've talked to everyone I've met or even heard of. It's as if someone told them not to help me. Yet, they've brought us food, visited with me and the children, offered advice on every topic but one. All they can suggest about finding employees is to talk to Ryan Walker.''

Again he said nothing.

''I know you don't care about helping me, but please think of those two little children who have already lost their parents. Must they lose their home also?'' She bit her lip to hold back the tears that threatened.

''I'm not the one who's telling everyone to send you to me. It's those damn women!''

''What are you talking about?'' she asked, irritated by his response.

''Mabel, Florence, Edith and Ruth. They've been arranging marriages around the county for several years now. First they got all their sons married. Then they started helping out their neighbors.''

''But surely they wouldn't try to ruin us. That's not fair to Josh and Mandy. Please, can't you help us?''

''Lady, I don't know of anyone to hire. If I did, I'd hire them myself. I'm shorthanded.''

''But you loaned me Doug and Hinney—''

''I know. I'm not stone-hearted. But I've got problems myself. I can't spend all my time worrying about your problems.''

''If one of them is Beth, I'll be glad to baby-sit her. My place is closer than town. It would save you some time.''

''Yes, it would. But I need someone to cook and clean my house, too. I'm going to hire a housekeeper.''

''Have you found one yet?''

"No. I'm getting the same treatment you are."

"Oh." Suzanne didn't know what to say. Finally she asked, "So tomorrow is going to be the last day Doug and Hinney come to my place?"

He gave her an exasperated look. "Don't stare at me with those big chocolate eyes. I don't have any answers."

"But—" she began. But he cut her off.

"Go home. I'll do some thinking about it tonight. In the morning I'll tell you what I'm going to do. Maybe I'll even have an answer for you. Right now, I need to think."

Since she had no other choice, Suzanne nodded and went back to her car. She drove back to the Howe ranch, trying to figure out what he'd meant. Life would be so easy if she could take on the job of housekeeper, taking Josh and Mandy with her to his house and coming back home at night. Maybe she'd suggest that tomorrow morning.

She actually relaxed as she realized that would take care of all their problems. She wouldn't take a salary and he could take care of the ranch. It even sounded like a fair trade to her.

Okay, in the morning, she'd explain her inspiration and all her problems would be solved.

RYAN PACED the floor until late into the night. The fool thing about it was that Mabel and Florence's solution was the best one. From what the men said, the McCoy woman was a great cook. She was doing a good job with the children, and the house appeared clean to them. All the things he needed.

She also seemed happy with her lot in life. She wasn't planning on running back to the city. She'd told them she was staying for the children. He could place Beth in her care without a worry. All he had to do was let her into his life.

As painful as that sounded, he supposed he could do it for Beth's sake. He'd be rewarded with a clean house, decent food and a happy Beth. He'd even get his fair share of sex. It had been a while since he'd—best not to think about that.

He finally accepted, at least in theory, that marrying Ms. McCoy would be the smart thing to do, but he still couldn't picture himself going through with it. He saw himself in his dusty jeans and worn boots, watching a football game on a Sunday, while she sat beside him in one of her suits, her makeup perfect and her hair untouchable, reading book reviews and finding art galleries for them to visit.

Damn! He'd be miserable. And so would she. It was ridiculous!

Then he'd start the logic all over again, trying to convince himself that marriage to Suzanne McCoy was the right choice. By four in the morning, he was punch-drunk with lack of sleep. He decided to wait until six o'clock, another two hours, before he told her what he had decided. Then he could come home and fall in bed for a couple or three hours.

Until then, he would pace the floor some more.

Chapter Three

Suzanne had been getting up at six-thirty each morning, even though the children slept until seven. That gave her time to have their breakfast ready. It also meant she had a few minutes of silence to gather herself for the long day.

This morning she didn't intend to change her routine, but a pounding on the front door at six had her leaping from the bed in a panic, afraid there was an emergency. She grabbed her robe and threw it on as she ran for the door.

She gave no thought to her appearance. Something was wrong. She needed to find out what and deal with it. She swung the front door open and came face-to-face with Ryan Walker.

"What's wrong?" she asked urgently.

"Nothing," he answered, his voice slightly slurred. "Everything's all right."

"Are you drunk?" she asked, staring at him.

"No. Just worn out. I haven't been to sleep." He leaned against the doorjamb and Suzanne thought he was going to fall.

"If nothing's wrong, why are you banging on my door?"

"I said I would."

Suzanne swept back her long hair and Ryan followed the gesture with his gaze, making Suzanne conscious of her appearance. "Come on in. I'll get dressed and make us some coffee."

He stumbled in and she led him to the kitchen. He sat down at the table and she quickly filled the coffeepot. Then she turned to excuse herself to go change and discovered him sound asleep.

"Mercy," she muttered. According to her neighbors, this man was her savior, the key to her finding men to work the ranch. But she was beginning to think he was crazy. Without waking him, she hurried to her bedroom. Five minutes later, in her usual jeans and shirt, she began making a breakfast that would satisfy any man. Bacon, sausage, biscuits and scrambled eggs.

When she was finished, she dished it all up, with a steaming-hot cup of coffee, and awakened her gentleman caller.

"Mr. Walker, breakfast is ready."

He raised his head and stared at her blankly.

"Drink some coffee," she said, nudging the mug closer to him.

He did as she recommended. Then the full plate in front of him inspired him to pick up his fork and eat. He hadn't had a breakfast like that in a long while. He didn't speak again until the plate was empty and he was almost out of coffee.

She stood and picked up the coffeepot. He automatically stuck his cup out for it to be filled again.

"Good breakfast."

"Thank you. I hope it helps you make sense. Why did you come pounding on my door at six o'clock? And is someone staying with Beth?"

He blinked several times. "Hinney is taking care of Beth. She likes him."

"Good. Okay, now answer my question."

"I give up." His simple statement didn't furnish her a clue, but he appeared to think it explained everything.

"I beg your pardon?"

She got up to refill her own cup, stalling for time to figure out what he meant. "I don't understand."

"I said I give up. You win."

"So you realized what I thought of, too?" she asked, thinking he'd come to the same conclusion as she had. "Thank goodness. Now, I'll come over every morning at seven and cook the children's breakfast at once. Then, I'll have dinner ready for you and Beth when you get in, and the kids and I will come home. It should work well."

She jumped up to get some paper and a pen. She was a list-maker and this change in her lifestyle definitely called for a list. "I won't come Saturdays, but you can bring Beth here if you want to for the day. That will give her a change of environment which I think will be good."

He stared at her blankly. "You look different."

That was enough of a non sequitur that it stopped Suzanne's list-making. "What?"

"Where's your suit?"

"You want me to wear a suit and heels to work as a housekeeper?" She couldn't agree to such a ridiculous request.

He cocked his head sideways, his blue eyes looking cloudy, as if his eyesight was no clearer than his head seemed to be. "No. No suits."

He seemed quite clear about that. "Fine, I didn't want to wear a suit." She returned to her list now that the suit thing had been settled. "Now, shall we start today? Or do you want to wait until Monday? Either way is fine with me. But we might run a little late today because I don't have the children's breakfast fixed."

"Today? Nope. Wouldn't be legal."

Suzanne scratched her forehead. What was he talking about? "Do housekeepers require a license around here? Do I have to take a test? I assure you I can cook and clean. And I'm doing a good job with Josh and Mandy. Beth shouldn't be a problem."

"Need a license."

"Uh, okay, I'll take care of the license. Why don't we wait until Monday to start? You go home and get some rest. Okay?" she asked, trying to keep a cheerful smile on her face.

"Okay," he muttered and pushed himself from the table as if it took all his energy to move. "Good breakfast."

"Thank you."

She followed him to the front door, not at all sure

he'd make that distance, but he seemed to get his second wind.

"Will you be able to drive?" she asked warily. She didn't want to drive him home.

"Yeah. Okay." Then he stumbled over to his truck, got behind the wheel and drove away.

Well, working for him would be strange, if he was like that all the time, but at least she'd found a way to save the kids' inheritance. That was what counted.

Suzanne heard the children waking and hurried to the kitchen to fix their breakfast. When they'd finished eating, she told them she was going to work as Mr. Walker's housekeeper and they would go with her each day.

"I suggest you take out your little suitcase, Josh, and pack a spare set of clothes and any of your favorite toys you might want for the day. We're going to start going there on Monday. I'll pack a little case for Mandy," she added, smiling at the little girl.

"Me pack," Mandy assured her. She was moving into the terrible twos, Suzanne had decided. She wanted to do everything herself.

"Fine, but first, I want you to practice your colors this morning. And Josh is going to practice his numbers. Okay? Go wash up and get everything we need."

She cleared the dishes while they did their chores. She wondered if Beth had had any practice with her numbers or her letters. She'd have to see once they got started. But she'd have to proceed carefully. She wouldn't want to upset the little girl. The drastic change in her routine was going to be difficult enough for her.

She began making her menu for lunch while the children finished their work. They had been working quietly for about an hour when the phone rang.

"Hello?"

"Suzanne, this is Mabel Baxter. Congratulations, I'm so happy for the two of you."

Suzanne thought the woman was a bit effusive given the circumstances, but she was glad they'd worked things out, too. "Well, thank you, Mabel. Yes, I'm pleased."

"You'll need to get the license right away, you know."

"Yes, that's what Mr. Walker said."

There was a distinct pause. "You call him Mr. Walker?"

"I guess I could call him Ryan, but I don't want to be too forward."

It sounded like the woman was choking.

"Mabel, are you all right?"

"Yes, of course, dear. I just wanted you to know that we'll help. We're quite experienced in these things."

"Well, that's very nice of you. An extra cake, or a pie occasionally would be greatly appreciated."

Another small silence. Finally, Mabel said, "We'll talk later dear, when you're more organized."

After saying goodbye, Mabel hung up the phone and Suzanne stared at her receiver. Finally she hung it up, too. Why had Mabel sounded so strange? She liked her. She'd visited her this week, along with Edith, one of the other ladies Mr. Walker had mentioned.

Would he want her to call him Ryan? In Dallas, most housekeepers called their employers by their last names. She didn't want to appear too familiar. She'd best stick to Mr. Walker.

That settled, she continued with her planning.

IT WAS TEN AFTER THREE when Ryan finally woke up. He'd been wakened several times by Beth. He'd gotten up to fix her lunch, and another time to pour her a glass of water, but mostly he'd dozed. He felt much older than his thirty years when he forced himself awake as Beth shook his shoulder. "Daddy?"

"What, sugar?" he asked, slowly sitting up.

"I need a snack. Millie gives me cookies or something."

"Uh, okay, sugar, I'll find something for a snack." He rolled out of bed, feeling a little more human than the last time he'd been disturbed.

Before he could reach their pantry, the phone rang. Beth screamed, "I'll get it!"

He vaguely remembered a phone call when he'd just gotten back from the city lady's place. Damn! He'd agreed to marry her! What was wrong with him? He decided he'd best answer the phone. "I've got it, Beth."

"Hello?"

"It's Mabel Baxter, Ryan. Remember you said

you'd get the license today so we could hold the wedding Sunday?''

"Vaguely," He muttered.

"Well, it's already three-thirty and the county office closes at five. And I'm not sure the bride-to-be understands what's going on. What did you tell her?"

"Mabel, I was up all night without any sleep. I may not have made myself clear."

"You'd better have. We're having a wedding Sunday afternoon. The whole town is pitching in."

"Mabel, damn it! I told you not to make a big deal out of it." In fact, he'd hoped to marry without anyone noticing.

"It may be your second time down the aisle, Ryan, but for that young lady it's her first and only time. We want her to enjoy it."

"Yeah, but I've got to go if I'm going to get the license in time."

"I know. But don't forget you'll need her along with you," Mabel warned him as he hung up the phone. He stood there for a minute. Then he dialed the number for Suzanne McCoy. When she answered, he didn't even tell her who it was. "I'll be there in ten minutes to take you to get a license."

"But Ryan—I mean Mr. Walker—I called. There is no license needed for a housekeeper. But I promise I'm qualified."

"We're getting a license to get married. Be ready!" And he hung up the phone.

SUZANNE MCCOY was still holding the phone to her ear, arguing with a dial tone.

"Susie, is something wrong?" Josh asked.

"Uh, I don't know. A misunderstanding, I think." She hoped that's what it was. Marry the man? He was crazy. And it wasn't necessary. Her plan would work.

She'd been giving the house a spring-cleaning all day. She wouldn't have much time for cleaning it when she worked all day with the three children at his house. Someone knocked on the front door and she stared at her watch. It couldn't be Mr. Walker. It had only been five minutes.

She hurried to the door and discovered it had been longer than she thought. There he stood, an impatient look on his face. He had Beth in his arms. She pushed open the screen door. "Come in."

He came in and set Beth down on her feet. "Are you ready?"

"No, I'm not. I think you've got things all wrong. I didn't agree to marry you. I agreed to be your housekeeper. I'll come every day and leave after you get in for dinner."

"No. We're getting married."

"How can you say that?"

"I can say that because half the town will be at our wedding on Sunday. Can Al take care of the kids for a couple of hours?"

She took a step back, frowning. "No. He's out with Doug and Hinney. So I can't leave."

"I'll go get him. In the meantime, you get ready.

Oh, and Beth is hoping you have a snack for her. Our pantry was bare.''

She stared in exasperation when he turned on his heel and walked out. Her gaze encountered Beth's hopeful blue eyes, so like her father's.

Suzanne sighed. ''Come on, Beth. The kids are having their snack now. We'll join them.''

''What are they having?''

''Ice cream with fresh strawberries and a little whipped cream on it.''

Beth's eyes widened in excitement. ''Oh, boy! I think I'll like that!'' She skipped along beside Suzanne.

In the kitchen, there was a fast introduction to the other children while Suzanne made the treat for Beth. Then she turned the television on to *Sesame Street*. ''I may have to go out, but if I do, Al will be here. But I want you to watch *Sesame Street* until it's finished. Okay?''

All three children nodded, their eyes already glued to the television. Suzanne continued her job of rubbing down the cabinets. She was sure she'd be able to convince Ryan he'd misunderstood. She certainly had.

Ryan was feeling a little better about his forthcoming marriage. After only seeing Suzanne in suits, he'd now seen her when she first woke up in her nightgown and robe, her hair flowing free, and he'd seen her in jeans. She looked damn good in jeans. Maybe the side benefits would make this marriage tolerable.

But there seemed to be some confusion in her

mind. She thought she could sashay around his house every day as a housekeeper, and everything would be all right? What would happen when other men saw her in jeans? He'd have visitors tramping through his house all day. She'd get marriage proposals, and if she accepted one, he'd have to start all over again. But if he married her, she'd have to only flirt with him. Only be married to him.

He liked that idea.

He found the men and told Al to get in the truck, because he needed him to baby-sit. His men were doing okay, so he didn't bother to explain anything. There wasn't time.

"I'm happy to baby-sit a little while. Your men are hard workers. I have trouble keeping up."

"I know what you mean, Al. But we'll always have a job for you."

Al nodded, as if he expected such an assurance.

When they got back to the ranch and Al discovered he'd get ice cream, too, he was happy. After serving him, Suzanne nodded to Ryan and led the way out of the kitchen. "We have to talk," she said once they were in the hall.

He tugged her kerchief that held back her hair off her head. "No, there's no time. We have to get the license this afternoon."

"Ryan, if you'll just listen, we can avoid marrying. I'll be the housekeeper you need. You can handle Beth at night, can't you?"

"It won't work that way. There will be whispers and all kinds of talk. And you'll have other men wanting to marry you. If that happens, Beth would be upset and I'd be in trouble again. And what if the man you marry isn't a rancher? You'd still need help.''

She stared at him. ''But—''

''It's the only way. I fought it myself for a long time, but in the end, there was no other answer. That's why the ladies of Cactus succeed so often at matchmaking. They're so damned good at it.''

''I can't believe—''

''Just come with me to get the license. We can discuss it again before Sunday, but the more you try to argue against it, the more you'll see a marriage of convenience works.''

She fell silent and though he watched her out of the corner of his eye as they drove to the county courthouse, she said nothing else.

Inside, she filled out the necessary information and watched when he put down the required money.

''Good thing they don't still require the blood tests. That would take more time.''

''Yes, that's true, but since it's a marriage of convenience, a blood test might not be necessary,'' she said.

He shushed her at once. ''Hey, don't spread that around. We'd be the objects of gossip for the entire year. That's no one else's business.''

''I'm sorry. I didn't think.''

Once they got the license, she assumed they'd head back home. Instead, he suggested they dine at the Last Roundup, a big restaurant on the town square. ''Cal Baxter's wife, Jessica, owns it.''

She protested. "I don't have dinner made for the children. They'll be hungry soon."

"I'll call Al. He can make them a peanut butter and jelly sandwich or something. They'll be fine." He gave her a smile. The first one she'd seen from him. *Oh, dear,* she thought to herself, *I'm in trouble. He's so handsome when he's smiling.* She looked away.

"I really think we should just go on home."

"Nope, we've got to celebrate our nuptials."

"I didn't think it was something you wanted to celebrate," she accused, watching him.

"I've learned to make the best of bad situations."

"What a compliment," she pointed out, coming to an abrupt halt.

"Don't stand in the road, sugar. You'll get run over." When she didn't budge, he scooped her into his arms and didn't put her down until they reached the sidewalk.

"Ryan, I'm not dressed for dinner out. I've been cleaning the house all day. I can't go in that fancy restaurant."

"It's not that fancy," a deep voice said behind them and Suzanne spun around to find Cal Baxter, the sheriff, standing behind them, his hands on his hips. "Jess won't throw you out 'cause you're wearing jeans. That's pretty common around here."

"But I've been cleaning the house all day," she continued to protest.

"Then you deserve to eat out. Come on. Jess and I will join you if you don't mind."

Suzanne felt she didn't have any choice but to

agree. She glared at Ryan. "Fine. I'll just call Al about what to fix for supper for the kids."

"There's a phone right inside the door," Cal said and led them up the steps.

By the time Suzanne had called Al, telling him about the cold roast beef she'd planned for sandwiches the next day, Cal had them a table toward the back of the restaurant. Since the restaurant was fairly full, she was surprised at how quick he'd been.

"It's the family table. They always keep it empty, in case we want to eat. When you're married to the boss, there have to be some perks," he added with a grin.

"True," Ryan agreed. "You'll have a few perks married to me, Suzanne."

She didn't answer, hoping Cal hadn't heard. She should've known better.

A beautiful dark-haired woman joined them. "Hello, Suzanne. I'm Jessica, Cal's wife...and Mabel's daughter-in-law. I hope you'll speak to me in spite of that."

"Oh! Of course. I don't blame Mabel and Florence, but—well, I guess I might as well say it...I find this situation hard to believe. We're expected to get married on Sunday?"

"Yes, you are," Jessica said, with a grin that made her even more beautiful. "We were the first of the ladies' many successes. One of *them* even married. Florence was a widow and she and Doc, well, he's actually our medical examiner, got married."

"My, life must be exciting around here."

"Actually," Jessica replied, "we settle down into a nice routine most days."

"Yes, I like routine. I think it's especially important for children. I'm the guardian for Josh and Mandy Howe."

"Yes, and thank goodness you'll also be taking care of Beth. We've all worried about her because Ryan is a heathen. You'll have to watch his vocabulary."

"I've noticed."

"Hey! I watch my tongue around Beth. It's the cowboys that say the wrong thing."

"I thought you were a cowboy?" Suzanne asked.

"I am, but—oh, never mind," Ryan said.

"I had to learn to watch myself, too, once the babies came," Cal said.

"How many children do you have?" Suzanne asked Cal.

"Two little boys," Cal answered with real enthusiasm that impressed Suzanne. "They're the greatest! My mom and dad spoil them rotten, of course, but they also help us take care of them. With my job as sheriff and Jess's restaurant, we're pretty busy."

When Suzanne looked at Jessica, expecting the same enthusiasm, she found her staring at her napkin, saying nothing. Was something wrong?

Then two more people came in and joined them. They were introduced as Mac Gibbons, a lawyer, and his wife, Dr. Samantha Gibbons.

"You're the lawyer who handles the finances for the children!" she exclaimed.

"That's right. I thought you'd be in to see me right away," Mac said, just before he gave his order.

His wife, a pretty woman with a warm smile, looked at Jessica and nodded her head. Suzanne looked at Jessica, too, and saw the happy smile she'd been looking for earlier. What was going on?

Samantha leaned over to Suzanne and whispered, "If you need any kind of birth control before the wedding, I'm working in the morning."

Chapter Four

Before Suzanne could pull herself together to respond to Samantha's offer, Jessica stood and leaned over to whisper in Cal's ear. He stood also, and followed her from the table.

Everyone stared at Samantha.

"What's going on?" Mac asked.

"Is something wrong?" Ryan asked.

Suzanne didn't ask anything. She thought she might even be able to guess what had just happened. She waited.

"So, is everything ready for the wedding?" Samantha asked. That took Suzanne by surprise. "How did you—"

"Florence is my mother-in-law."

"Oh. I didn't realize everyone was connected in this town."

"Yes, I'm afraid so. Have you figured out what to wear yet?"

"No. I'm not even sure I can go through with it," Suzanne said without thinking.

Ryan protested indignantly, "Hey!"

"You said we could discuss it again!" she reminded him. "I don't think marriage is necessary."

"I don't know," Mac said slowly. "We're a pretty conservative town. Living together isn't very accepted."

Suzanne turned a bright red. "No! I mean, I intended to be his housekeeper, but I would go home to the children's house each night."

"It won't work," Ryan said flatly, staring at her.

"I still don't see why," she said.

"Because of the kids. They all need a permanent situation to make them feel safe," Mac said. "And you need a permanent solution to the ranch problem. Cal told me that you fired all your men and hadn't found anyone to replace them."

She knew he was being kind in not adding that she wouldn't know a good cowboy from a bad one.

"Yes, but—okay, maybe you're right, but what if Ryan meets his soul mate next year, when he's married to me? What happens then?"

"Well, he can divorce you. In which case, hire me as your divorce attorney and we'll strip him bare," Mac promised, with a chuckle. Everyone laughed except her and Ryan.

Cal and Jessica returned to the table, and Jessica asked, "What are you laughing about?"

"We're planning how Suzanne and I will take Ryan to the cleaners if he tries to divorce her next year," Mac explained cheerfully, as if that were normal conversation.

Jessica looked at each of them. "Oh. But he's a

very nice man, Suzanne. Are you sure you want to divorce him?''

"You didn't hear about him and Lola? I thought gossip was rampant in Cactus," Suzanne said, getting into the spirit of the conversation.

Jessica looked from Suzanne to Ryan and said, "Oh, you and Lola, huh? I'm on your side, Suzanne."

"Wait a minute. It was Lola's fault!" Ryan protested, going along with their teasing. "She seduced me!"

"Just like a man," Suzanne said, "always blaming it on the lady."

Everyone chuckled.

"But seriously, Suzanne, have you figured out what to wear?" Samantha asked again. "Because we all have dresses and we'd be glad to loan you one."

"Well, I do have a very nice cream suit. Would that do?"

"A suit?" Ryan asked, unhappy with her choice.

"Yes. It's a nice suit."

"I think that sounds lovely," Samantha said. "And I have a cream hat with a small veil. I'll bring it out to you tomorrow after office hours."

"Oh, thank you, Samantha."

"Who are you going to have as your maid of honor?" Jessica asked. "I'll volunteer. After all, I've known you five minutes longer than Sam."

"I'd be pleased if you would," Suzanne said, feeling much better.

"What's your favorite color?" Jessica asked.

"Blue," Suzanne replied, careful not to look at Ryan's eyes. She certainly hadn't chosen that color because of his eyes. Of course not. "Could Mandy and Beth be flower girls? And Josh the ring bearer?"

"Perfect!" Samantha said, clapping her hands. "Now, we need someone to give you away. Cal? You're the law in these parts. Do you feel up to the job?" She suddenly turned serious. "Unless your father…" she said, looking at Suzanne.

"No. If Cal doesn't mind, that would be wonderful." She looked at Ryan, who seemed uninterested in their discussion. "Who will your best man be, Ryan?"

"Well, I was going to ask Mac, but if he's going to be *your* divorce attorney, I don't know." Ryan lifted an eyebrow in her direction, drawing attention to his blue eyes.

"Oh, all right, I'll find another divorce attorney."

"You can have Alex. She's a damned good attorney. And she's my partner." Mac looked at Ryan. "You may regret that decision, because Alex might be even more vicious."

"Naw. I'd rather have a male attorney. Besides, there won't be a divorce," Ryan said.

"By the way, I ordered for us when Cal and I were in the kitchen. We have something to celebrate tonight," Jessica said, changing the subject. "We're having another baby."

Even Suzanne cheered that announcement. It was clear how much they cared about each other.

''Cal said no more babies, but I wanted to have a little girl. So keep your fingers crossed for us.''

They all cheered. Dinner was much more enjoyable than Suzanne had expected. When they left to head home, she felt that she had made two good friends. In the truck she said, ''Everyone is so friendly here.''

''You met some of Cactus's best people tonight. There are some others, too. We all went to school together,'' Ryan said. ''I was a few years behind them. And then I married Tiffany.''

''Is that Beth's mother?''

''Yeah.''

''Beth is such an old-fashioned name compared to Tiffany.''

''That's because Tiffany didn't have any interest in naming our baby. She was mad because she'd gotten pregnant. I named her after my mother.'' The bitterness in his voice was clear.

''I'm sorry,'' Suzanne murmured.

''You'd better be good to Beth. She's suffered enough because of her mother.''

Suzanne turned in the seat to stare at him. ''The same goes to you. You'd better be good to Josh and Mandy, too. They're great kids but they need a daddy to love them.''

''All right. So we'll each be a parent to the kids, okay? See, things are working out, aren't they?''

Suzanne swung around to stare out the truck window. She hadn't set out thinking she'd actually marry Ryan, but somehow the evening had been spent planning their wedding, two days away. "I guess so," she said softly with a sigh.

"Good." He replied and neither of them spoke again the rest of the way home.

The children were very tired and a little unsettled that Suzanne and Ryan were out after dark. Suzanne sent Josh off to the main bathroom while she took Mandy to the other one for a quick bath after telling Ryan and Beth goodnight.

"Did you have fun tonight?" she asked Mandy.

The little girl leaned against Suzanne's arm and said, "I like Beth."

"Good. I think you'll get to play with her a lot soon."

"Okay," Mandy said, her eyelids slowly going lower. Suzanne got her out of the bath and dried her off. She felt bad about not telling the children about the wedding. But she wanted to wait—to be sure it would really happen. It seemed so make-believe to her.

THE PHONE STARTED ringing early the next morning. Jessica had decided to throw her a shower. Suzanne was stunned. "But Jessica, the wedding is tomorrow."

"I know. That's why we'll have the shower tonight. Melanie and Alex are going to help me. You haven't met them yet, but you will this evening. It will be fun."

"But I don't know anyone here!"

"Maybe not, but most everyone knew Mary Lee and Rodger. We liked them both. And we're glad the kids will have a good home. So just think of it as a tribute to your cousin and her husband. Does that make it easier?''

With tears in her eyes, Suzanne agreed. What else could she do? ''Thank you. That's very sweet of you.''

''Okay. Ryan will pick you up at seven. Bring Mandy and Beth with you. It's a girl thing. Ryan will take Josh with him to the bachelor party.''

Suzanne was stunned by that statement. ''Don't you think Josh is a little young for a bachelor party?''

''These bachelor parties are different. They meet at the restaurant and play darts. Ryan will take care of him.''

''If you're sure.''

After the phone call, Suzanne found a pretty dress in her city wardrobe that would be fine for the party tonight. Then she checked Mandy's closet. The only party dress Mandy had turned out to be outgrown. She called Ryan.

''Does Beth have a party dress?''

''Uh, I don't think so. Why?''

''Because they're giving me a shower tonight and the girls are supposed to go with me. Mandy needs a new dress. I thought I'd drive into town and see what I can find. Shall I buy one for Beth, too?''

''Would you know what size?''

''Of course not. I would need Beth to go with us.''

''Uh, okay. You want Josh to stay here with me?''

"I don't think he has anything to wear either. Would I be able to find a suit for him?"

"Maybe. But nice slacks and a white shirt would be dressy enough."

It suddenly occurred to her to ask about his wardrobe. "You *are* wearing a suit tomorrow, aren't you?"

"Of course I am. They were just joking about me being a heathen, Suzanne."

"Would you have Beth ready in about half an hour?"

"Yeah."

She should've checked with Mac about the children's allowance before now. Looking in Mandy's closet reminded her that Mandy would need more clothes. She'd apparently just had a growth spurt. When she announced to the children they were going into town with her to get new clothes, Mandy clapped her hands, even though Suzanne wasn't sure she understood what she was going to do. Josh frowned at her.

"Why?"

"Mmm. Well, I have something to tell you. Mr. Walker and I are—are going to get married tomorrow."

Both children stared at her. Josh finally said, "What happens to us?"

"Sweetheart, you'll come with me wherever I go. We're family. We're just going to have a larger family. You and Mandy and Beth will be our children." No response. She asked, "Will that be okay?"

"So we'll live in his house?"

"Yes."

"Who will live here?"

That question hadn't occurred to Suzanne. "Josh, I don't know. I suppose we could rent it out, but— we'll ask Mr. Walker, I mean Ryan, when we go pick up Beth."

"We're going to take Beth with us?"

Uh-oh. "Don't you like Beth?"

"She's bossy."

"We'll work things out. But she's used to being an only child. It may take her a little while to get used to having a brother and sister."

Suzanne tried to discuss cheerful things after that. But when they got to Ryan's place, she remembered Josh's question. "Ryan, who will live in the house on our place?"

"I was going to ask you about that. I've got a good man who deserves to be manager. But I've already got a manager. I thought I'd make him manager of that land and let him and his wife live there. They're expecting a baby soon and don't have much room where they're living. Would that be all right?"

"Yes, of course. Did you hear, Josh? Some people who are going to have a new baby."

"A boy baby?"

Suzanne looked at Ryan. He squatted down in front of Josh. "Yeah, Josh, they're having a boy baby. Another cowboy."

"Good. My daddy was going to teach me to be a cowboy. But now he can't." Josh's sad eyes almost made Suzanne break into tears.

Ryan, however, took care of the situation. "No, he can't, but I can. Want me to teach you?"

"Even how to ride?"

"Well, of course. Riding is the first thing to learn."

"Daddy said it was too dangerous for me to learn now."

"But you're older now. You'll take to it right away. After things have settled down, I'll show you how."

"I can ride," Beth announced, looking triumphantly at Josh. He scowled in return.

"Beth rides with me some. But I'll teach you together."

Though Suzanne was concerned about the safety factor, she was grateful for Ryan's offer to Josh. "That's very good of you, Ryan," she whispered before leaving with the children.

"It's no better than you taking Beth shopping." He opened his billfold. "Here's some money."

"No. I'll charge it and you can pay me back later. I don't know how much it will be." Besides, she would pay for her own wedding. Even if she didn't want one.

Four hours later, she knew Beth a lot better, including her stubbornness, which Suzanne was sure she got from her father. But overall, she was a sweet little girl who played well with Mandy. In fact, Beth acted like Mandy's mother, and Josh tried to corral both of them. Suzanne found herself looking forward to spending time with all three children.

She'd found the girls dresses for the wedding,

matching pale-blue dresses. And she'd bought them simpler dresses for the shower this evening. When she told Josh he'd be going with Ryan, he hesitated. Then he asked, "Ryan won't mind?"

"Of course not. Maybe he'll show you how to throw darts."

That cheered him up.

She bought fast food for dinner, since she wouldn't have time to cook, clean up and get dressed for the shower. Not and get three children ready. She suggested Beth stay with them to get ready. Suzanne promised to fix her hair for her. "If we have time, I'll even paint your nails."

Beth was awed by that offer and if Beth liked it, Mandy clapped, too. Suzanne made a special note to paint nails.

At last they were all dressed in their new dresses and Josh in nice slacks and a blue dress shirt. At the very moment Suzanne thought she should maybe call Ryan, he knocked on the door.

Beth ran to the door, dying to show off to her father. When she opened the door, she beamed up at him. "Look at me, Daddy! Aren't I pretty?"

"Beth, a lady should wait until a man compliments her. Then she thanks him," Suzanne pointed out, but she was smiling.

"Okay, Daddy, tell me."

Ryan scooped Beth up and obliged. "You are absolutely beautiful. And Mandy is, too."

"Look at my nails," Beth said, practically sticking them in her father's eyes. Mandy, standing on the floor and looking at the man and her new friend, held up her nails for him to see, too.

Ryan dipped down and picked Mandy up with his other arm. He admired her nails as well, telling her she looked beautiful also. Suzanne drew a shaky breath. Damn the man. He always knew what to say to the children. He was a good daddy.

"Hey, Josh, don't tell me you got your nails painted too?"

"No, sir. That's girl stuff."

"Yeah, but you do look nice tonight. So everyone's ready to go? Even Mom?"

"Susie," Josh snapped. He always insisted she be called by her name and not Mama or Mom. She hadn't warned Ryan because it hadn't occurred to her that he'd call her such a thing.

"Susie? I like that name, Josh. Think she'll let me call her that, too?" Ryan asked, giving nothing away with his smile.

Josh nodded his head, not looking at anyone.

Suzanne leaned down and kissed Josh's cheek. "You behave yourself tonight, okay? You have your bag packed to spend the night with Ryan?"

"Yeah," the boy said gruffly, and Suzanne wanted to hug him close, but she didn't want to break his fragile dignity. "Okay. I've put your clothes for the wedding on the hangers. Mind Ryan and I'll see you tomorrow." Then she stared at Ryan, trying to signal him to be gentle with the little boy. He'd been through so much.

"He'll be fine. Cal is bringing his two boys tonight and Tuck has a little boy who's coming.

Spence's boy is a baby. He'll be at the shower. Oh, and Gabe and Katie's little boy is coming, too.''

''There'll be other boys there? I don't know many boys around here.'' Josh's eyes were large.

''Yeah. There's lots of kids around here. If you like 'em, we can invite them over sometimes.'' Ryan took his hand. ''Come on, let's get out of this place. It smells like girls.''

''Yeah,'' Josh said, trying to imitate his attitude.

Ryan led Josh to the door. Then he looked over his shoulder. ''By the way, Ms. McCoy. You're the prettiest one of them all.'' And he was out the door.

Suzanne caught her breath in her throat. He looked pretty spiffy himself, but she hadn't said anything.

She appreciated his care towards Josh even more than the compliment.

THE NEXT DAY at two o'clock, Suzanne stood in the back of the church, unable to believe she was going to walk down the aisle and marry Ryan Walker. It would solve both their problems, but she was so afraid it would create so many more.

A tug on her skirt reminded her of the two little darlings standing beside her. Beth was waiting for her attention.

''There's lots of people in there.''

''Don't worry. They'll be thinking you and Mandy are absolutely beautiful. I'm so proud of you both.'' Then she noticed Josh wasn't there. ''Where's Josh?''

''He said he had to see Daddy,'' Beth told her.

Cal stepped into the bride's room. "Is everyone ready?"

"Apparently Josh went to see Ryan. Do you know where he is?"

"Sure do. I'll go find him. By then it will be time to go down the aisle. By the way, you're a beautiful bride."

"Thank you." Her suit had a V-neck and sparkling buttons down the front. The skirt was short and she wore cream stockings and heels. And she wore the chic hat Samantha had loaned her. She'd done her best to look like a bride. She'd even pulled down the cream netting on the hat.

Cal returned with Josh.

"Sweetheart, is everything all right?"

"Yep. I had to tell Ryan something."

"All right. Well, it's almost time." She nodded to the lady playing the organ and she switched to the "Wedding March."

"Okay, girls. Put the rose petals on the floor the way we said." She gently pushed the two girls forward.

Jessica, who'd been fixing Suzanne's hair, said, "I'll be right behind you girls."

The two little girls started down the aisle, holding hands.

"How will they sprinkle rose petals while they hold hands?" Jessica asked in a whisper.

"It doesn't matter," Suzanne assured her. When the girls got to the end of the pews, Mandy pulled her hand free and grabbed a handful of petals and dropped them on the floor. Then she looked at her basket and turned it upside down. Beth started picking up the petals and putting them back in Mandy's basket. Ryan leaned forward and said something. Then Beth emptied her basket, too.

The pastor asked them to come stand by him while guarded chuckles ran through the audience.

Jessica went down the aisle next.

"Is this for real?" Suzanne asked Cal under her breath.

"Yep, it is. And everything's going to be all right," Cal assured her.

She clutched the bouquet Jessica had given her, saying it was a gift from Ryan. It was beautiful.

She walked slowly down the aisle, her gaze fixed on the handsome man waiting for her. He was wearing a suit as promised, and was the most handsome man in the room. Josh was just in front of her, handling his duties with poise. She hadn't thought about buying a ring for her new husband. She didn't even know if he'd wear one.

What a beautiful mess.

When they reached the altar, Cal handed her off to Ryan and sat down in the front row. Suzanne turned to face Ryan and he took her hands, bringing them to his lips. "You're beautiful," he whispered.

Okay, so he knew what to say to make her feel better. But those blue eyes were incredible.

Then she realized the minister had begun the service. It was too late to pull back. She was getting married.

RYAN THOUGHT the church looked great. There were candles and flowers. And lots of people. Almost two hundred people had turned out to celebrate their wedding. He appreciated their efforts. He hoped Suzanne did. She was still a little shaky about everything.

Before they had left for the shower, she'd cried last night when she was telling him about how wonderful all the women were to her. He could read anxiety in Suzanne's brown eyes. He'd put his arms around her for the first time and liked how it felt. He'd liked taking Josh with him last night too. The boy was worried about all this change and trying not to show it. Waiting at the altar, Ryan realized he, Suzanne and the kids were going to be all right.

The music changed, and he looked up to see Suzanne enter the room in her cream suit. Wow! That suit didn't make her look efficient or formal. It made her look sexy. And her hair was left down on her shoulders, its fiery glints dancing around her. He drew a deep breath. After helping the adorable flower girls to their places, he concentrated again on Suzanne. He nodded to Josh as he took his place. Then he took Suzanne's hands and kissed them.

''You look beautiful,'' he whispered. The tears that popped into her eyes surprised him and worried him. But she began repeating her vows at the minister's direction, and he realized he really was getting married again. He'd vowed never to do so.

He gave Suzanne a ring to slide on his finger. He noticed her surprise, but he wanted to wear a ring, just as he wanted her to wear a matching band. He slipped it on her finger and held her hand firmly in his.

Then they reached the magic words, "You may kiss your bride." Their first kiss in front of everyone. He caught a note of surprise in Suzanne's eyes just before his lips touched hers. The sweetness of that kiss would stay with him for a long time.

Chapter Five

"Ladies and gentleman, may I present Mr. and Mrs. Ryan Walker," the minister said. "They request your presence at the reception to follow at The Last Roundup."

Ryan led Suzanne down the aisle. "Now you're going to meet every citizen in Cactus. At least it will seem like it. You okay?"

"Yes," she said faintly.

He was moving quickly because they were supposed to get to the reception first so they could greet everyone.

A photographer ran ahead of them and shot a picture of them. Suzanne frowned. "Are we big news?"

"No, I hired him to take pictures. Didn't you notice him in the church?"

"No, I didn't. I hope he got one of the girls as they went down the aisle. Didn't they look sweet?"

"Yeah. I think they're going to get along pretty well."

"Yes, but I worry about Josh. He's still hurting and—"

"Don't worry. He'll become a cowboy."

"But I want him to be safe."

"Let's not have our first fight now. We'll save it for later."

She didn't say anything.

"Are your shoes comfortable? I told you you look great, didn't I? I thought you meant a business suit."

"Yes, thank you. You look very nice, too."

"We're a virtual admiration society, aren't we? Here we go," he said as they reached the reception and he swung her around. She saw everyone in the church heading their way and took a deep breath.

An hour later, they greeted the last of their guests and Ryan led her out onto the dance floor. His arms slid around her and she leaned against him for only a minute. She was so very tired.

"Are you all right?" he asked softly.

"I'm a little tired. I didn't get much sleep last night, and the girls got up early this morning."

"I bet they kept you busy. Josh was a perfect gentleman. He came in and sat on the floor by my bed, waiting for me to wake up. It's unnerving to wake up and find someone staring at you."

"Yes, I can imagine." She straightened and followed his dance moves.

"I like dancing closer. Anytime you want to lean against me, feel free."

She drew a deep breath. "No, thank you, I'm fine."

"Suzanne, it will be okay. We're going to have a good family."

"I hope so."

He pulled her closer and swept her across the floor to applause from everyone around them.

Suzanne was so amazed at the smoothness of the wedding and the reception. When Ryan went to get her a cup of punch, Jessica and Melanie stopped to talk to her. "But I don't understand. How can all this be organized so quickly?"

"Practice," Melanie said. "Our mothers-in-law have done this so many times, I think they could do it in their sleep."

"Well, I certainly appreciate all the work. I know you two did a lot, too, with the party last night."

Jessica laughed. "As Melanie said, it's become second nature now. Everyone has a recipe for things for a shower. And Katie's bakery handles the wedding cake and things for a reception. I have this room, and the setup is easy. In fact, I think Cactus should be the wedding capital of Texas."

"But if it were, don't you think single men would avoid it?" Suzanne asked.

"You've got a point there. But usually, the ladies have figured an angle that makes the decision completely logical. They did that for you, didn't they?" Melanie asked.

"Yes," Suzanne agreed with a frown. "It is logical, for the children. I'll admit that Ryan seems to understand the kids. He's very good with them."

"Yes," Jessica agreed. "His wife, that is, his first

wife, was no good at anything but pampering herself. We felt so sorry for him.''

''Where did she come from?''

''One of our marriages brought a millionaire into our community. Well, he was already here, but he was hiding. After the marriage, he began developing some industry here for the town to grow. Tiffany's father had one of the big jobs. Tiffany found Ryan and charmed him into marriage.''

''She must've been beautiful,'' Suzanne said.

She hadn't meant to sound wistful, or jealous or whatever Melanie heard. ''You're more beautiful,'' Melanie said.

Suzanne smiled. ''You're so sweet, Melanie. But you know we're marrying for the children's sake, and no other reason. I don't expect anything from Ryan.''

Melanie and Jessica exchanged a look that Suzanne couldn't understand.

''Just give the marriage a chance,'' Jessica murmured.

''Yes, of course,'' Suzanne assured them. What else could she say?

When the time came for them to leave, they gathered up the children. Josh had been playing with the friends he'd made the previous night. The two little girls had stayed close to Suzanne or Ryan. All five of them told everyone goodbye, Suzanne holding Josh's hand and Ryan carrying a little girl in each arms. Then they went outside.

''My car is here. The girls' car seats are in it, so I'll drive the children back.'' Suzanne suggested.

"I'll take Josh in my truck. I'm glad they packed food for dinner for us. You'll probably need to do some grocery shopping first thing in the morning. I haven't had time lately."

"We have some food at our house that I should stop and collect. It will just go bad if I don't. Is that all right?" Suzanne asked.

"Yeah, sure. But why don't you bring the children to the house. I'll look after them while you get whatever you need. That would be easier, wouldn't it?"

"Yes, if you don't mind."

"We're a family, Susie. Don't forget that."

She said nothing else. It was the first time he'd called her Susie, and it made their relationship seem much more intimate. Unlike a marriage of convenience.

But she knew that was what they had.

She actually stayed at his house long enough to put the two girls down for a late nap and tell Josh that he had to have some quiet time, too.

He protested, but Ryan quietly said, "A cowboy has to mind his mama, son. And whatever you call her, Susie is going to be your mama. I don't ever want to hear that you did anything disrespectful to her."

"No, sir," Josh said.

To soften those words, Suzanne walked Josh to his new room and hugged him. She also gave a critical eye to the room. "After we give this room a good cleaning, we'll bring over some of your favorite things to decorate it. It will feel more like home, then.''

''Thanks, Susie,'' he said, his eyelids drooping. Though he considered himself too old for a nap, she knew the day had been stressful. A nap would be good for him. She tiptoed out of the room.

Ryan had hired a couple of cowboys to come in yesterday and clean the house. But it had been neglected for a long time. Suzanne realized she had a lot of work ahead of her.

''Well, the children will be fine until I get back,'' she said, stopping at the door of the kitchen to tell him.

''Wait a minute. I'm going to call Doug to come baby-sit while they're sleeping, and I'll go with you. You might have something heavy for me to carry.''

''I can manage.''

''I'm coming,'' he said emphatically. She didn't bother to argue. It didn't much matter, so why fight over it?

Five minutes later, Doug was established in the kitchen with the paper to read, and Ryan, after receiving congratulations from Doug, led Suzanne to the truck.

''Shouldn't you change clothes?'' he asked before he backed out of the driveway. He was in jeans and boots again, instead of his suit.

''I left my suitcase at the house. I'll change after we get there.''

''Why didn't you bring it with you?''

She stared straight ahead. ''In case it didn't happen. I'm finding it very hard to comprehend what happened today. To have such a huge wedding in three days, to marry a man I don't really know. It's hard to grasp all that at once.''

''But it's a done deal now, Susie. We're married and we're going to stay that way.''

She said nothing. She couldn't argue that fact. But accepting it wasn't easy. When she got to the house, she opened her suitcase and took out jeans, a shirt, tennis shoes and socks. ''I'll go change if you'll start boxing up the food in the pantry.''

He nodded and she escaped to her bedroom. Though she'd only been there a little over a week, it seemed so much more friendly than Ryan's house. She supposed, though his house was larger and nicer, it felt unlived in because he and Beth only slept there each evening. Between his work and Beth's staying with his cousin, they didn't put much into the house.

But she could turn the house into a home. That she could do. Her only concern was turning a wedding into a marriage, after all, Ryan was practically a stranger to her. He was going to save the ranch, and she was thankful, but she wasn't sure she was prepared for the intimacy of marriage.

She repacked the suitcase and carried it out to the kitchen. ''Have you finished the pantry?''

''Nope. You've got a lot of food here.''

''It takes a lot of food to make a varied menu that will tempt children.''

''I'm not complaining. I'm looking forward to being on the receiving end of that varied menu.''

While Ryan worked in the pantry, Suzanne turned

her attention to packing the food from the refrigerator. They finished about the same time. While he carried the food to the truck, she went back to Josh's room and took down some of the drawings and pictures Josh had on his bedroom wall. Adding them to his room at Ryan's would make it seem more like his room.

"Suzanne?" Ryan called from the kitchen.

"Yes," she answered as she came from the back of the house. "I'm ready."

"I put your suitcase in the truck also. Do the children have their clothes and things at my house?"

"Most of it. We'll need to come back tomorrow to get anything I missed."

"Okay. I won't let Dick and his wife move in 'til next weekend. Will that work for you?"

"Yes. I moved some of my kitchen utensils yesterday, but there's more I'll need. You seem to be lacking those things."

"What are you talking about? I've got a frying pan and a big pot."

"Yes, and that's all you've got. Never mind," she added when he opened his mouth to argue with her. "I'm too tired to discuss it tonight. And I'll take care of it myself tomorrow. Or the next day."

He put an arm around her shoulders and led her out to his truck. "Everything doesn't have to be done in a day or two, Suzanne. If you need more time or some help, let me know, okay? You don't have to carry the weight of the world on your shoulders."

She didn't say anything.

Back at home, he carried things in and she began putting food away. Then she took out the leftovers that had been sent home with them and organized a cold meal. The children were still sleeping, but Suzanne decided to wake them up.

On her way down the hall to their bedrooms, Suzanne passed the master bedroom. She noticed her suitcase sitting by the open door. She guessed Ryan didn't know which bedroom she'd use. She'd already scouted out the house. The only other available room was across from the children's. It was small and only had a day bed, but she could manage until she could buy a full-sized bed. She put her suitcase in there.

They all sat down, she and Ryan and the three children, for their first meal together. The children were still tired, but they didn't fuss with each other. Mandy climbed into Suzanne's lap halfway through. She continued to eat a little when Suzanne fed her like a baby bird, but she fell back asleep after a few minutes.

Suzanne left her half-eaten meal and carried Mandy to Beth's room. The two were sharing, Mandy's bed having been put in the room with Beth's. She washed Mandy's face and hands, which didn't even waken the child. Then she dressed her in pajamas and tucked her into bed.

When she returned to the kitchen, the other two children had finished eating and were ready for bed. Ryan told her to sit down and finish her meal and he would tuck those two in. Suzanne started to insist on doing the job, but she changed her mind. He was a parent, too.

And she was hungry.

After she ate, she cleaned the kitchen. First the dishes. Then she took a mop to the tile floor. She was surprised to find the tile was a pearl-gray, buried beneath a lot of dirt.

When Ryan came in, he stopped in surprise. "Hey! Nice job. But you shouldn't be working tonight. You had a full schedule today."

"I wanted to do it. I like my kitchen spotless."

"I had the boys come in and clean up for you, but I guess they didn't do such a good job."

Suzanne smiled wearily. "I'm sure they tried. But the house has been neglected for a while because you couldn't do ten jobs at once. I'll work on it."

"Why don't you call it a day early tonight?"

"In a little while. I want to get everything ready for breakfast in the morning," she said, her mind already making a mental list of what she needed to do.

"Honey, I'll eat with the boys in the morning. You sleep until the kids wake you up." He took the mop out of her hands and turned her toward the bedrooms. "Go soak in the tub and get ready for bed."

"A shower. Do you have a shower?"

"Sure, I have one. There's not one in the kids' bathroom."

"Then I'll use your shower. But I'll be quick."

"No hurry. I'm going down to the bunkhouse to talk to the guys about what we're doing tomorrow and how we're going to handle the extra herd and land.''

''Okay,'' she agreed, grateful to have the house to herself.

The shower made her feel good. Almost not exhausted. But even a shower wasn't that miraculous. She scooted out of Ryan's bathroom. It connected his bedroom to her small room. Maybe they could work out a routine where she could use his shower every night while he visited with the men, or watched a program on television or something. She put on a nightgown and robe. Then she dug into the linen closet and found a sheet and a blanket. She stole the extra pillow from Josh's bed. She was making up the small bed in her little room when she heard Ryan return to the house. He called her name a minute later.

''Yes?'' she returned.

Heavy steps came down the hall. ''What are you doing?''

She straightened from putting the last touch to her little bed and smiled at him. ''I was making up my bed.''

''This isn't your bed,'' he said flatly, almost daring her to argue with him.

''Yes, it is. It's the only bedroom left.'' She stared at him, wondering what emotion he was feeling. It didn't look pleasant.

''You're sharing my bedroom. We were married today, remember?'' His hands were on his hips and his jaw was squared.

Suzanne stared at him. "Yes, we were, but we both agreed it was a marriage of convenience."

"And you think that means…?" He waited for her to finish his sentence.

"That we have a partnership that doesn't include sex," she said bluntly, not wanting there to be any mistake.

"No sex? For how long? Do you want me to court you? Or do you want time to get used to everything?"

"What are you talking about?" Suzanne replied. "You said a marriage of convenience. *You* used the words first."

"Damn it! It's not convenient for me to go without sex for the rest of my life. That's ridiculous!"

"Well, I didn't agree to sleep with you whenever you feel the need for sex! You said we got married for the children, not for convenient sex!" Her hands went to her hips and she glared at him.

They were at a standoff. She was tired, but she couldn't afford to lose this argument. She'd agreed to a marriage, but not that kind of marriage.

He began pacing, and ran his hand through his hair. "Damn it, Suzanne, I can't promise to go without sex forever. I'm a man!"

"That much is obvious or we wouldn't be having this argument," she said, trying to keep her voice even, though she felt like screaming.

"Are you saying you have no desire for an intimate relationship? You're not attracted to me?"

"Ryan, I barely know you. Surely it takes more

time than we've spent together to build a—a need for each other.''

''Not for me. You're attractive.''

''So is the Leaning Tower of Pisa, but you don't—''

''What does that have to do with anything?'' he demanded.

She couldn't take any more. Her body swayed. ''I have to get some rest. Can't we argue about this tomorrow?''

''We'll be arguing about it from now 'til Christmas, Suzanne. This is unacceptable.''

''Fine! Just go away so I can get to sleep!'' she cried. She fell down on the small bed and leaned against the wall. ''Please?'' she added in a soft voice.

''Fine! But we *are* married!'' With those words, he stomped down the hall, into his bedroom and slammed the door.

Ryan Walker was not a happy man.

Chapter Six

They didn't talk the next morning. As he'd promised, Ryan had breakfast with his men, accepting a lot of teasing about being up early after his wedding night.

He withstood it and tried not to let his grumpiness be obvious. When he got home that evening, the kitchen was cleaner than it had been in years. A pretty tablecloth with real dishes on it decorated the table, and the meal was as good as he'd ever eaten.

The children were happy and discussing what they'd done during the day. Beth showed him some pictures she'd colored. Of course, as soon as she did, Mandy scooted down from the table and got her pictures, too. It seemed Mandy followed Beth everywhere. Ryan asked Josh about his work and he showed him his papers. Then Josh asked Ryan what he'd done on the ranch that day, hungering for ''man talk.''

Ryan knew how Josh felt. Man talk was easier to handle. His covert looks at Suzanne showed him nothing but a calm surface. No personal feelings.

And she didn't show him what she'd done that day. But it was obvious in the kitchen. When he went in to say goodnight to Josh, she obviously also had cleaned his room and added some of his things to the walls.

"Did Susie work on your room today, Josh?"

"Yeah. She did it while the girls went to sleep."

"Do you like it better now?"

The boy nodded.

"Josh, I want you to tell me if you get unhappy or something's wrong. We may be able to fix it with not much work, so just tell me, okay?"

"That's what Susie says, too."

"Good. We want to be a family."

"Well, there is one thing," Josh finally said.

"What is it, pal?"

"Could you and Susie have a boy baby? Then I'd have someone. Mandy and Beth stick together all the time."

Ryan sat there, his brain whirling, thinking about Susie having his baby. Finally he cleared his throat. "There's no way to be sure you get a boy. We might have another girl."

"Oh. Well, I guess I could stand that."

"Um, we'll have to wait and see. We all need to settle in first. And, um, don't mention that to Susie, okay?"

"Okay."

When he escaped Josh's room, he went in to kiss the girls goodnight. First he kissed Beth. Then he kissed Mandy. His daughter sat up in her bed.

"I don't want you to kiss Mandy!"

"Why not?" he asked, sitting down on the side of Mandy's bed.

"Because you're my daddy. Not hers."

"That's not true, Beth. Do you let Susie kiss you goodnight?"

"A'course. She loves me."

"But she's not really your mother."

"She's not Mandy's mama either."

Mandy's eyes filled with tears. Ryan took her in his arms and held her close. "Don't cry, Mandy. Beth is not being nice, but she didn't mean to hurt you."

"Why is she crying?" Beth asked, a little bewildered.

"Beth, you don't remember your mommy leaving. But Mandy remembers her real mommy and she misses her. Susie is a good mommy, but Mandy still misses her real mommy. And you just reminded her she's gone."

"I didn't mean to do that, but I don't want to share you." Beth's jaw squared and her chin lifted. Ryan recognized the symptoms of his daughter digging in her heels...just like he did. That gave him pause for thought, but he couldn't think about it now. "Then Mandy won't share Susie with you."

"But I told you, Susie loves me. She said so."

"And I love Mandy," he said, kissing the little girl again as Mandy snuggled closer to him.

Beth crossed her little arms over her chest and pouted for a minute. Then, she smiled. "Okay, we'll share." And she flopped down in her bed and closed her eyes.

He tucked Mandy back in and made sure she would go to sleep just as quickly. Then he slipped from the room with a sigh.

He wanted to tell Suzanne about his experiences with the kids, but she'd disappeared from sight. Since the door to the room she'd taken was closed, he assumed she didn't want any conversation. He wished he could change her mind as quickly as he had Beth's, but no such luck.

In the kitchen, he found a note saying she'd serve him breakfast in the morning. That was it. He went to bed alone, missing her presence in more ways than one.

AFTER A SILENT but tasty breakfast the next morning, he went to the bunkhouse to make sure everyone knew his assigned task for the morning. Then Ryan got in his truck and went to town. He wanted to see Mac about handling finances for the children's place.

Mac was there early, as usual, and they clarified everything easily. He was about to leave when Mac said he was going over to Katie's shop and have a cup of coffee and a cinnamon bun. Ryan decided to join him.

"Cal usually comes out when he sees me cross the square, unless he's got something going on," Mac warned him. "Hope that's all right."

"Sure."

"I only asked because you don't have the look of a happy newlywed," Mac continued, as if Ryan had asked a question.

Ryan came to a halt. "What do you mean?"

"Wait until I get some coffee down me. Look, here comes Cal now."

They didn't talk again until the three men were seated at a table outside the shop.

"I shouldn't be eating this. Suzanne made me a big breakfast this morning."

"Good. It will take away that lean and hungry look," Cal said.

Ryan said nothing.

Mac, however, leaned forward. "I was noticing he doesn't look so happy for a newlywed."

"Probably exhausted," Cal remarked, studying Ryan.

"Guys, come on, let's talk about ranching, or the law, or some criminals that have escaped."

"Uh-uh," Cal said, still staring. "So what's wrong, sunshine? What have you got to complain about now that you're getting some regular activity?" he asked with a grin.

"She says we have a marriage of convenience," Ryan retorted. "Convenient for her but not me." He slumped down in his chair and stared at the cinnamon bun.

"You mean she won't—" Mac stopped and scratched his neck. "That's tough."

"Didn't you explain why the two of you should…you know…?" Cal asked.

"I told her she was attractive," Ryan said defensively.

Silence fell. Finally Cal said, "Boy, you are dumber than rocks."

"Hey!" Ryan protested.

"Well, you are. Lots of women are attractive. You have to feel more than that before you get naked."

"I did all that sort of romantic stuff with my first wife. She laughed at me. Then she ran off with another man. I'm not going through that again." Ryan refused to meet either of their glances.

"Then you'd better prepare to do without," Mac said calmly.

"Would you even be *interested* in a woman who had sex with every fellow who's attractive. Around here, we call them sluts."

"No! And Suzanne's not like that."

"Of course she's not. We wouldn't have let you make that mistake twice," Cal said.

"So you knew Tiffany was—was a slut?"

"Yeah." Mac sighed. "We think Suzanne is real nice. Did you two discuss any of this before you got married?"

"There wasn't time. And I said it would be a marriage of convenience, but I didn't mean no sex. How can I go forever without having sex again? Especially with her around the house."

"So you'll have to open up your heart to her," Cal said.

"I can't!"

"Maybe if you give it a few weeks. Be friendly, give her time to get to know you."

"She doesn't want to. She runs and hides as soon as the kids go to bed."

"Be patient, Ryan. A good woman is worth the wait. We're fortunate to know that."

"Yeah. I know. But I'm not sure she'll—I mean should I apologize?"

"It doesn't hurt," Mac said. "I have to apologize all the time, but Sam forgives me. And eventually I learn."

"Okay. I'll go home and offer her some time. And ask her to talk to me, so we can get to know each other."

"Good," both men agreed.

Suddenly, Ryan had no interest in the cinnamon bun, or the coffee. He wanted to talk to Suzanne and straighten things out. "Uh, I'd better go."

"Sure." Mac nodded. "We understand."

Ryan took the roads a little fast, praying Cal wasn't on the road behind him. When he whipped into the driveway, he parked his truck and then sat still. How was he going to start a conversation if she avoided him? What could he say?

He decided to just blurt out the words if they would stop her from running away. He had to do something. He opened the door and went into the house.

The moment he stepped into the kitchen, he began apologizing. "Suzanne, I was wrong—"

That's when he realized there were two women sitting at the table while Suzanne poured glasses of tea at the kitchen counter. "Oh."

"Ryan, you know Mrs. Epihheart and her sister Louise?"

"Uh, yeah, sure. Hello, ladies. I just got back

from town and—and I'm going out to the barn. I'll talk to you later, honey.'' He whirled around and escaped out the door.

Damn, damn, damn! Now he'd have to worry about his apology the rest of the day.

SUZANNE FOLLOWED Ryan's path to the barn with her gaze. Her day had been difficult. She worried constantly about their situation. It had thrown her off-stride. How could she live like this, hiding in her room from dark until dawn?

Then she'd had unexpected visitors. The ladies had missed the wedding. They came to introduce themselves and brought presents. Of course, Suzanne was gracious and grateful. But she wanted to know what Ryan had been about to say. When the ladies left, she began preparing lunch. But she didn't know if Ryan would come in for lunch or not.

She called the kids to the table, setting a place for Ryan, too, in hope that he would come back. They had just begun eating when the back door opened.

''You got enough for me, too?'' he asked softly, surprising her.

She whirled around. ''Of course we do. Come in.''

''Here's your place, Daddy,'' Beth pointed out.

''I see. I'm glad I wasn't forgotten.'' He looked at Suzanne, a smile on his face.

She smiled back and suddenly found breathing a bit easier. They exchanged several smiles during the lunch. Then she served some chocolate cake. She was glad she'd managed to work in some baking that morning.

"Great cake, Susie," he said softly as she cleaned Mandy's face. The little girl had smeared the icing all over herself.

"Thank you, Ryan. Mandy, you need to take smaller bites. Then you wouldn't get so messy."

"Okay," Mandy said cheerfully.

"Beth, are you ready for your quiet time?" Suzanne asked.

"Yes, but I want Daddy to take me to quiet time," Beth said. "He can take Mandy, too."

"Is that all right, Ryan? Do you have time?"

"Sure, I can do it. Uh, will you be here when I get back?"

She was pleased that he wanted to talk to her. Maybe they could work something out after all. "Yes. I'll be cleaning the kitchen."

"Okay. How about you, Josh? Have you got something to look at while you rest?"

"Yes. Susie got me a new picture book about horses."

"Great. Once I settle the girls down, I'll stop by for a minute and look at it."

Josh's face brightened and he grinned at Ryan. "Great!"

Again Suzanne reminded herself that Ryan was a good man, and an even better father...to all three kids.

She cleaned the kitchen and still no Ryan. Finally, she sat down at the table, a cup of coffee in front of her and a second at Ryan's place. When he appeared in the doorway, she gave him a timid smile. She hoped for so much.

"I'm sorry I burst in on your guests this morning. I, uh, I had something on my mind and just didn't notice."

"That's all right. What did you have on your mind?" She clasped her hands together in her lap, where he couldn't see how tense she was.

"I wanted to apologize about…about the other night. I was unreasonable. I—I was looking forward to—well, you know. I didn't handle it well. I won't—I mean, I'd like us to get to know each other. To take time to see how things work out. But we can't do that if you hide from me. If I promise not to touch you, can we—talk, spend some time together?"

Involuntarily, her hands reached out across the table. "Oh, Ryan, I was so worried. I knew we couldn't continue like this. I've been worried, so tense—"

He caught her hands and kissed them. "I know. It was my fault. Last night, I wanted to tell you about the kids, but you were in your room and I was afraid if I knocked on the door, I'd scare you."

"I didn't know what to do."

"Don't say any more. The fault is all mine. Maybe we can spend some time together after the kids are in bed. By the way, I've noticed all the work you're doing around the house. And how the kids are learning every day. You're amazing!"

Suzanne's cheeks turned red. "I'm just doing what most mothers do. It's no big deal."

"I've been married to someone who didn't do any of it. It is a big deal and I want you to know I appreciate it."

"Thank you."

"Mac said you should come in to see him about the money. You haven't drawn any out of the kids' accounts."

"No, I have some money from the insurance I got when my mother died. I've been using it."

"Go see Mac in the morning. I can stay in and keep the kids."

He was still holding her hands. She pulled away, smiling at him. "I will. But I'll get Al to come over to baby-sit. He likes to get out of the sun and rest up a little. And I still have chocolate cake left."

"That ought to convince him. It's damn good chocolate cake."

"I appreciate the sentiment, Ryan Walker, but you've got to stop saying that word. Someday, Beth is going to come out with it at the wrong time and you'll regret it."

He grinned. "Okay, Susie."

"What did you want to tell me about the kids?" she asked.

"Uh…well, Beth protested when I kissed Mandy good-night last night. She didn't want to share me."

"I was afraid of that. It's hard when she's had you all to herself." She bit her bottom lip, and Ryan thought she'd never looked so cute. "I'll talk to her."

"Well, I pointed out that Mandy was sharing you. Beth insisted that you loved her. You wanted to be her mommy.'' His smile broadened. ''Good job, Susie.''

''But it's true. I do love her.''

''Yeah. I think that's what makes you special. You have a big heart.''

''Ryan, you have to stop saying such nice things. I'm not a saint.''

''No, I guess not. That red hair tells me that. But you only seem to lose your temper in really bad times. I don't deserve the patience you've shown me.''

''Ryan! Please. Is that all the kids said that worried you?''

''No. And I fixed Beth. She decided to share, after all. But I'll admit that Josh stopped me. I couldn't think of anything to say for a minute.''

''What did he say?'' She asked, her brow crinkling with worry.

''He asked me if we could have a baby boy so he'd have someone like Mandy has Beth.''

Suzanne paled and then her cheeks flooded with color. ''What did you tell him?''

''I told him these things take time.'' He paused, then reached out for her hands again. ''And that's what I'm telling myself. Is it a deal? Can we get to know each other?''

''I'd like that very much, Ryan. I may have given the impression that I'm sophisticated, but I'm not. I appreciate you offering me time.''

A knock on the door interrupted them. Ryan turned and looked at the door and saw one of his men standing there. ''Yeah, Frank, what is it?''

"We've got a problem, boss, and I wanted to ask what you want us to do about it," the man said apologetically.

"All right. I'll be right there."

The man turned away and Ryan stood. Then he bent down and kissed Suzanne's sweet lips. "I'll see you at dinner."

He walked out the door.

Suzanne stared after him. When Ryan turned on the charm, he was a dangerous man. She'd have to be careful. Very careful. Because if he came back in the door right now, she'd throw herself in his arms and beg him to take her to the bedroom.

Oh, yeah. She needed to be on guard.

Chapter Seven

Ryan thought all his troubles were over. That night, he and Suzanne sat in the den and talked about their day, discussed the kids and things they needed.

The next day, Suzanne went into town to talk to Mac. She also did some shopping for the children. But she asked Ryan to take them to town that evening and get all three children their first pairs of cowboy boots. Josh was ecstatic, figuring he was halfway to being a cowboy. But he didn't understand why the girls got boots, too.

Ryan let Suzanne handle that question. They had less time that night to be together. The children got into bed late. There was something on the news she wanted to see, so they scarcely talked at all. But he made up for the loss by putting his arm around her shoulders and holding her close during the news.

The next night, she asked him to teach Josh how to swing a lariat. They practiced outside until the light was completely gone. He enjoyed it, but it was hard to keep his mind off Suzanne inside with the two little girls.

The following night, she asked him to show all three children how to play checkers. And he was beginning to get suspicious. Was she going to think up a chore for him every evening so they couldn't spend time alone? He did as she asked, and Josh caught on pretty quickly, but Beth only partly did so. Mandy thought the object was to move the checkers wherever she wanted.

After the children were put in bed, he cornered Suzanne in the kitchen where she'd insisted she needed to do some baking.

"Why do we desperately need more desserts?"

"I'm freezing them so I'll have something in reserve in case I need it," she calmly explained.

Unfortunately, it made sense to Ryan. "And what am I going to teach the children tomorrow night? Chess?"

"Do you know how to play chess?" she asked, her smile brightening.

"Not enough to teach anyone. What's going on, Suzanne? I thought we were going to spend the evenings together?"

She stopped stirring the cake batter she was mixing. "What do you mean?" she asked, not meeting his gaze.

"I mean you've been deliberately finding things for me to do with the kids. Then you're too tired to stay up with me. Do you regret our agreement to get to know one another?"

"Do you regret yours? Because you're breaking it every chance you get," she said, heat in her words.

"What do you mean?"

"You said we'd spend time together talking. No touching. But you've been touching every chance you get."

Uh-oh. He *had* been touching her…and enjoying it. It was hard to keep his hands off her. "But, Suzanne—"

"While it may not be your choice to spend time with the kids, it is important that you do. They all love to have your attention. It's helping them adjust and feel like a family. And it gives me a break. I'm sorry you're so against it."

That made him feel like a heel. "I didn't mean I didn't like spending time with the kids, but I thought—I'm sure— What do you have on the schedule for tomorrow night?"

"I thought you could take them to see the baby colt that was born this afternoon."

"How did you know about him?"

"Al told me. I understand they're keeping him in the barn until Friday, so we could go see him tomorrow."

"Yeah. All right. Will you come, too?"

"Of course. I'm dying to see him."

"Okay. Have you finished up in here?"

"No, I need to put this cake in the oven. Then I'm going to make a dessert for tomorrow."

"What can I do to help?"

She stared at him, as if to be sure he was serious. Then she stepped over to the cabinet and picked up a packaged angel food cake. She took a big bowl and put them both in front of him. "Tear the cake into small pieces." She held up her fingers in a circle. "About this big."

He frowned. "Why?"

"Because it's part of the dessert I'm fixing." Then she began pouring the cake batter into three pans. "Oh, wash your hands first."

It was an easy task and they talked about a lot of things while they worked. But he didn't come close to touching her because he had a chore to do.

"This would be a good job for the kids," he commented.

"Yes, I would've given it to them, but you needed something to do."

He grunted, irritated with her scheming. But in spite of himself, he grew interested in the dessert he was helping to create. "Now what?" he asked after he'd finished.

"Get a big spoon and the bowl of strawberries in syrup from the refrigerator."

"You put strawberries in syrup? That doesn't sound good."

"In their own syrup, Ryan. They're frozen that way."

She bent over to put the cake pans in the oven and he gave her a long look. She still looked good in jeans. The temptation to give her a little pat was great, but he was getting the feeling Suzanne would assign him more chores if he didn't keep his hands to himself. He opened the refrigerator.

He brought the bowl back to the table. "Now what?"

"Pour the mixture over the cake and stir it around."

"Aren't you going to take over? You know I don't know how to cook."

"It's not really cooking. And besides, when I tell Josh that cowboys cook, too, he'll believe me if he knows you made a dessert."

"Is everything a lesson for the kids?" he grumbled.

"No. Sometimes it's a lesson for you, too." She gave him a sweet smile and began rinsing the dirty dishes she'd used to bake the cake.

"Okay, I stirred it up. Now what?" He was worried about asking her that question. Who knew what she'd say?

She handed him a bowl of whipped cream, he thought, but she called it Cool Whip, and another bowl filled with red Jell-O. "Empty these into the bowl and stir them in."

He did so. Then he waited for her to notice that he'd finished. He wasn't going to ask again.

She brought five dessert dishes over to him. "Nice job. Now, fill these and cover them."

"That's it? Don't you cook it or something?"

"No. A lot of yummy desserts aren't hard to make. It's a matter of getting the right ingredients. You did a good job, Ryan."

"I'm not sure it's going to taste good."

"It needs to blend overnight. You'll see at lunch tomorrow. And the kids will be impressed that you made it."

He silently filled the bowls, irritated by her maneuvering. Yet he'd enjoyed making a dessert, though he wasn't going to tell her that. Actually, he'd rather be in the den making out with her.

A quick look at Suzanne told him she was keeping an eye on him. She was still suspicious of him. Maybe it was a good thing she was keeping his hands busy. He didn't think he'd be too reliable about keeping his hands off her if he didn't have something to do.

Maybe she didn't like sex. He'd heard there were women like that. He'd never met one, as far as he knew. Even Tiffany liked it. But she used it to punish him when she didn't get what she wanted. He'd soon lost interest in having sex with her. After a short while, it wasn't making love, because she'd already killed any feelings he had for her.

Maybe Suzanne's way was best. Take it slow and easy. If he only knew for sure that at the end they'd both be satisfied.

She put the filled dessert bowls in the refrigerator. Then she covered the large bowl and did the same to it. "We'll serve it at lunch tomorrow. You are coming in for lunch, aren't you?" she asked.

He liked that she looked forward to his coming in in the middle of the day. Then she ruined his thoughts.

"The children like to see you at lunch."

"And you don't?"

"Of course I do. But the children—"

"I know. Everything for the children."

She rinsed the spoon he'd used. Then she turned around. "Thanks for the help. I'm ready for bed.

I'm not even interested in the weather tonight. When the timer goes off, will you take the cake out of the oven and cover it?'' He nodded and she slipped from the room, leaving him sitting at the table. He wandered into the den and turned on the weather. A farmer or rancher couldn't afford not to be interested in the weather.

He was glad he'd checked. Thunderstorms were heading their way, with the possibility of tornadoes. He'd better warn Suzanne the next morning. He didn't want her taken by surprise.

SUZANNE CAME to the kitchen in the morning smiling. It took a lot of planning, but she was keeping Ryan's touching in check. She had other activities planned for tonight. And the time that Ryan spent with the children was good for them. Ryan was such a good father.

As usual, she had his breakfast ready when he came in, starting off with a cup of coffee. Ryan was slow to wake up.

"Good morning."

"Yeah," he muttered and took another sip of coffee.

"Busy day today?" she asked as she poured herself another cup of coffee and sat down at the table across from him.

"Yeah, but I'll be in for lunch."

"It's not necessary if you can't make it," she said.

"Yes it is when you're serving my dessert. I want to hear the praise."

"But you thought it wouldn't be good."

"I've changed my mind. In fact, maybe I should take a little taste to be sure."

He thought she'd argue with him, but she smiled. "Go ahead, but just a taste."

He opened the refrigerator door and picked the bowl with the most in it. He took a spoonful and slowly let it dissolve in his mouth before returning the bowl to the refrigerator. "I'll be here for lunch," he assured her firmly, his eyebrows soaring.

She smiled again. "I thought you would."

"Here's another reason I'll be in for lunch," he added. He bent and kissed her lips before she could protest. Then he finished his breakfast and was out the door.

Then he stuck his head back in. "Oh, Suzanne, we may have tornadoes today. There's a storm cellar out here. If you actually see a tornado, take the children down in it. Okay?"

"Is it clean?" she asked doubtfully.

"It's safe," he snapped and disappeared again.

She sighed. Another thing to add to her list. Check out the storm cellar. She wasn't going to close herself and the children up in a small space that was full of bugs and snakes.

She turned the radio on to a local station that would give warning if there were tornadoes in the area.

In Dallas, they had a lot of warnings, and she'd seen one or two tornadoes in the distance, but she'd never experienced one close at hand. The thought made her a little nervous. She decided to pack an emergency lunch, sandwiches and cookies. Maybe some fruit. Water and soda to drink. She'd leave the emergency rations on the cabinet, easy to grab.

She dug out a cooler so the sandwiches wouldn't be ruined. The kids got up for breakfast and she had packed the lunch by the time they finished eating.

"Kids, I'm going to the storm cellar to see if it needs cleaning out. You are to watch *Sesame Street,* and stay in your chairs until I get back."

She lined up three small chairs in front of the screen. "Even if the phone rings, stay in your chairs. Josh, I've put the phone right behind you so you can answer it without moving. Okay?"

"Yes ma'am," he answered, but it was clear his mind was on Big Bird.

She shrugged her shoulders. She hoped she wouldn't be gone long.

She was pleased to find that for a storm shelter, Ryan's was nice. He'd put in flooring, with a built-in bench along the wall on three sides. There was even some lightweight flooring in solid sheets covering the walls. It looked clean. But the smell of earth was overwhelming.

If the kids brought a pillow and blanket each, they could even take their nap down there. And there was a box of bottled water in one corner.

With the lunch she'd packed, everything would be fine. She hurried up the stairs, anxious to get out of the cellar. She wasn't claustrophobic, but she didn't like the idea of being underground.

The children hadn't moved when she returned to the house. She moved over to sit by the radio, kept low so it wouldn't disturb the children's program. Everything seemed okay so far. Then she gathered three pillows and three blankets and folded them. She piled it all by the door.

Probably nothing would happen, but she wanted to be safe, not sorry. A direct hit from a killer tornado would destroy everything.

"Here's a local warning. Several tornado clouds are in the area. Be sure you're prepared in case one of them hits the ground. We'll give you first word on it here."

Suzanne was glad the radio ran on batteries. She'd take it with her if they went into the shelter.

When *Sesame Street* was over, she told each child to get a storybook they liked. She gathered up some coloring books and the box of crayons. It would be best to keep things as normal as possible.

"We're getting these things together in case we go down into the shelter. I want you to have some things to do. And I've packed up a scrumptious lunch. When I say we have to go, take your book and climb down into the cellar. Josh, can you carry Mandy's book? And when you get down, turn around and help Beth and Mandy, okay?"

"Okay, Susie. What's a tornado?"

"It's a big wind. But it can't hurt us if we're in the cellar."

"But where will Daddy be?" Beth asked.

Suzanne had been dreading that question. She didn't have an answer that made her happy either. "He's taking care of the cows. He and his horse will get in a low place and the wind will go right past him. He'll be okay.''

"Okay, folks," the radio announced. "We've got one on the ground west of Cactus. It looks like a big one. Take cover at once.''

She couldn't believe it. She took a deep breath and said a silent prayer. "Okay, kids, let's try out our storm cellar.'' She smiled and led the children out the door and pulled back the slanted door of the cellar.

"Josh, you first. Be careful.''

The little boy took his sister's book and Beth's too, and climbed down the ladder. Beth went next and Josh helped her down. Mandy had more difficulty, but Josh was very good with her. "I'm going to get the lunch. Everyone stay down there, no matter what.''

Inside, she grabbed the cooler and carried it down the ladder. "Now, I'm going to get some blankets and pillows.'' When she came back out of the cellar, rain had begun. She grabbed the pillows and blankets and, shielding them with her body, she tossed them ahead of her into the shelter. Then she pulled the door, closing out the sound of the wind and rain.

"Oh, no, I forgot the radio!''

"I don't think you should go,'' Josh said.

"I have to. You're in charge, Josh, until I get back. Okay, girls?''

This time, the rain was coming down in sheets and she could see nothing. She tucked the radio under her arm, trying to shield it from the rain, and scrambled back down into the shelter, her clothes soaked.

''Well! I'm glad we're all safe. I didn't manage as well as I thought I would. If I had, I'd have brought a spare set of clothes for everyone.''

''We didn't get wet,'' Josh pointed out. ''Why don't you take off your clothes and wrap yourself in a blanket?''

''That's good thinking, Josh, but it's not cold in here, so I think I'll be all right.''

''What's that funny smell?'' Josh asked, wrinkling his nose.

''Oh, that, that's earth. See, we're underground. But Ryan has made it a nice cellar. Some people just have a hole in the ground. So, shall we color?''

She pulled out the coloring books and the crayons and spread out a blanket on the floor. ''You can lie on your stomachs and color.''

''Okay,'' Beth agreed, ''But when do we eat? I'm hungry.''

''We're going to wait a little while. It's not time to eat yet. How about I give you two cookies each? That would keep you going for a little while, wouldn't it?''

The children cheered. She gave them their snack and helped them pick pictures to color. They were busy and happy, which was good. But she was frightened and worried. Would Ryan find a place to shelter from the storm?

What if he got hurt? What if…no, she wasn't going to think that. She said a silent prayer for his safety and tried to concentrate on the children's work.

But it wasn't easy.

Chapter Eight

There were several tornadoes in the area, so even after the first one had gone, Suzanne didn't feel she should let the children leave the shelter. They had a picnic in the shelter. The little girls were happy. Josh, however, objected to the smell.

"We're lucky Ryan put lights in here," Suzanne told him. "This is a very nice cellar." She put the pillows on the floor. After having them all lie down, she covered them with another blanket. "Probably when you wake up we can go back in the house." She kept her voice cheerful, though she feared the house might not be there.

When all three kids had closed their eyes, she quietly climbed the stairs and released the door. Then she pushed it open an inch so she could peek out. Though it was still raining and the wind was blowing hard, she could see the house, standing strong in the storm. She breathed a sigh of relief.

"What is it?" Josh asked in a whisper.

"I was checking to see if the house is safe. And it is."

"Good. It kind of feels like home now."

"Yes, it does, doesn't it?"

She climbed back down the steps after latching the door again. "Can't you sleep?" she whispered.

"I'm kind of worried about Ryan."

"I know. But he's a smart man. He'll take care of everyone."

"Yeah. He can do everything."

She nodded but sat silently. Finally Josh's eyes closed. His even breathing took over and she knew he'd finally gone to sleep.

No more pretending to be cheerful. She could worry in peace. Worry that the grand plan to make a family might never get off the ground….

Half an hour later, she'd dozed a little, sitting on the bench, leaning against the wall. A loud pounding woke her up. The pounding continued and she sprang from the bench to the ladder, scurrying up it to release the door. Ryan's worried face looked down on her.

"Thank God," he muttered, pulling her up into his arms. He kissed her even though it was still raining. But she was so glad to see him, to know he'd survived, she didn't care.

"God, I've been so worried about you!" he exclaimed.

"Us? We've been safe and sound in here. You're the one who's been in danger. What did you do? Hide behind a tree?"

"We never saw a tornado. Just wind and rain. Did you?"

"No. When they said there was one on the ground west of Cactus, I brought the children down here."

"Good. I was afraid you wouldn't like it."

"Ryan, it's a very nice cellar. It even has lights."

"You can thank Tiffany for that. She refused to come down here unless it was nice."

"I never thought I'd be grateful to Tiffany, but I am."

"Hey! We're getting wet," Josh called up, rubbing his eyes.

"Ryan's here."

Josh struggled to his feet. "Are you okay, Dad?" Josh called up.

Both adults recognized the significance of his words. Ryan called down, "I'm fine, Josh, except I'm a little wet."

"Can we come out?" Josh and Suzanne asked together.

"Yeah. But you'll get wet."

Suzanne went back down the steps to get the girls. Josh scrambled up the stairs.

Ryan helped Josh out and told him to run for the porch.

"You're coming?" the boy asked, anxious.

"Yep. As soon as we get Mandy and Beth up here."

Josh ran for the porch. He didn't go in the house, however, but stood there, watching for the rest of his family.

Ryan took Beth in his arms as Suzanne passed her up. Then he waited to help Suzanne and Mandy out of the cellar.

"Is it all right if I leave everything in there until it stops raining?"

"Yes, it's fine."

They made it to the porch and then into the house.

"Josh can you go change clothes by yourself?" Suzanne asked.

"Yeah, but my boots got wet. Did I ruin them?" The little boy's expression reflected a major disaster.

"No, son, you didn't ruin them. Just take them off and let them dry before you put them on again. Okay?"

He nodded and hurried down the hall.

"I'll change the girls and tuck them in bed. I'm not sure they ever woke up," Suzanne said.

"No, Beth is awake, aren't you, honey? I think we should all meet in the kitchen and have the dessert I made…and celebrate making it through the storm."

She met his gaze, understanding what he was saying. "I think you're right. Come on, Mandy. We need to put on dry clothes. Then we're going to have more dessert. Won't that be fun?"

Suzanne and Ryan went to the girls' room and changed Beth and Mandy into dry play clothes. Then they sent the girls into the kitchen and headed to their own rooms for dry clothes. "See you in five minutes," Ryan said, giving her a quick kiss. She didn't even bother to protest.

"We get another dessert?" Josh asked as soon as the adults came in.

"Yes, Ryan made it last night."

All three children stared at Ryan. Finally Beth

said, "You can cook, Daddy?" There was a lot of doubt in her voice.

Mandy said, "Daddy cook!" willing to accept that statement as she heard it. She clapped her hands and beamed at him.

Josh wasn't as thrilled, but he said, "Dad can do anything, even cook."

"You're right," Suzanne said, opening the refrigerator. She brought the bowls to the table, asking Josh to get enough spoons for all of them.

"Guys, it didn't have to be cooked. And Mom told me what to do. But it's good. I've already tested it. I thought it would be a good idea to celebrate surviving the storm. I kept calling you and got no answer. I was afraid something had happened to you."

Suzanne gasped. She hadn't thought of the portable phone. How he must've worried. "I didn't think—"

"You'll remember next time."

"Hey! This is good," Josh exclaimed, surprise in his voice.

Ryan's gaze met Suzanne's and they both smiled. Mandy didn't bother to approve. She just kept eating. When she finished, she banged her bowl on the table and said, "More!"

Beth ate her dessert slowly, staring at it. "Did you really make this, Daddy?"

"I really did. It's easy to make. Susie will show you how."

"Really?" she asked, her gaze going to Suzanne. Suzanne nodded.

"Goody! Then I can cook, too."

When the children were tucked in bed, Suzanne came back into the kitchen. Ryan stood there. He wrapped his arms around her. "Today is one I won't long forget," he whispered against her temple, holding her close. "I want you to know, Susie, I'll wait as long as it takes. But we're a family. Okay?"

"Yes. We are a family. And I appreciate some time, Ryan. I have adjusted as quickly as I can, but three weeks ago, I worked in insurance in Dallas. Now I'm a rancher's wife with three children."

"That is a big change. Instant family. You did well today, keeping the babies entertained in the cellar. I'm proud of you."

"I'm sorry I didn't take the phone."

"It might not have worked anyway."

She moved out of his grasp. "I need to put things away." Ryan had gone down into the cellar and brought all their things up.

"I'll help."

"Okay. We'll put them away together."

The work was quickly done and they returned to the kitchen for a cup of decaf coffee.

"Tell me about your life in Dallas," he said softly, staring at her.

"It was boring," she assured him.

"I still want to know."

SUZANNE FELT a little better about their situation after that day. Ryan spent time with the children and talked with her at night, not trying to trick her into his arms. But he wanted to know about her life. She'd begun asking him questions, too.

One night about two weeks later, they were all sitting around the table, enjoying their dessert. They had the back door open. The screen door kept out the bugs, but allowed the breeze to come through.

"Well, well, well, if it isn't the little family," a cool female voice said.

Suzanne whipped her head around to see a woman standing on the porch, staring at all of them. Somehow, she wasn't surprised when Ryan identified the woman.

"Tiffany! What are you doing here?"

"I came to pick up my child," Tiffany said with a smile. She opened the screen door and stepped into the kitchen. Ryan said nothing. Suzanne was sure he was in shock.

"Which one is she?" the woman asked, looking at Mandy and Beth, sitting beside each other.

Suzanne was shocked by that question.

"It doesn't matter. You're not taking her away," Ryan said in stern tones.

"Why not? I'm her mother. You've had her for a while. It's my turn."

Suzanne spoke quietly, "Children, please go to your rooms and read for a while." Her voice was warm but firm. She didn't want Beth to hear the woman.

The children must've sensed something, because none of them spoke. They slid out of their chairs and hurried out of the room.

"Come on, Ryan. You used to be fair."

"I am fair. You don't deserve to take Beth away. You abandoned her when she was six months old, and you didn't even care. No child should be exposed to that kind of treatment."

"I've changed my mind."

"You can't even recognize her!" he protested, his voice rising.

"So, I'll take either one of them. It doesn't matter."

Suzanne gasped, but said nothing.

"What's going on, Tiff? Tell me the truth."

"My husband wants a child. I can't have another child, and adopting takes too long."

"Sorry."

"I didn't think you'd agree. You always were so sentimental. But I've got plenty of money and I'm taking you to court, Ryan, darling." She pulled a folded paper from her purse. "See you in court. Oh, and pack her stuff." Then she walked out of the house.

"Can she get custody of Beth?" Suzanne asked, her heart aching. It would be terrible.

"I'll go see Mac first thing in the morning. I'll fight her with everything I have. She doesn't care about Beth. She just wants to keep her husband and his money."

"I do feel sorry for her not being able to have more children." Suzanne thought how she would feel if she couldn't have children. But this woman had been so cruel to her husband and child.

"She's not going to get her. And don't let her in

the house ever again, whether I'm here or not. I'll leave a gun here.''

''A *gun?* You want me to shoot her?''

''I want you to keep her from stealing Beth...or Mandy. It's likely she'll try. Don't let the kids go out without you. This is very important.''

''I know that, Ryan, but I've never shot a gun. I wouldn't know how to use it.''

''I'll show you. Damn, damn, damn. I should've gotten her to sign a paper back then, when she didn't give a damn about Beth. But it never occurred to me that she'd change.'' He laughed harshly. ''But, of course, she hasn't. She's as selfish as ever, expecting the world to conform to her desires.''

He stomped off to his bedroom, slamming the door behind him. Suzanne went to the children's rooms to talk to them, make sure they weren't upset.

''Who was that lady?'' Beth asked.

''No one you need to know, sweetheart. No matter what she tells you, don't go near her, okay?''

''Okay. And Mandy, too?''

''Yes. Neither of you should go away with her.'' Suzanne decided she'd teach the girls how to call home tomorrow.

''Are you ready to go to sleep?'' she asked them.

''Will you read us a story?''

''Of course I will.'' She sat on the bed and the girls crowded around her. After she'd read the book, she tucked each of them in her bed and kissed them goodnight. ''I'll see you in the morning.''

Josh had a few more questions she didn't want to answer. She asked him to help her keep an eye on the girls, to keep them safe. He immediately agreed. She gave him a hug and a kiss.

When she had them tucked in, she went back to the kitchen. Ryan's door was still closed. Was he regretting his divorce? She didn't see how anyone could love such a woman, but he once had. Maybe he still loved her. He wanted Suzanne. She knew that. But then, he'd apparently gone without sex for three years. He'd never mentioned love.

She locked the back door. Then she checked the front door. When she went to bed, she left her door open slightly, to hear if anyone came in the house. It took a long time to go to sleep that night. Hopes of their becoming a happy family seemed distant tonight.

RYAN WAS WAITING for Mac when he got in the next morning. "Do you have any appointments this morning?"

"Why? You want to go fishing or something?" Mac asked with a grin.

"No." His voice was solemn, but inside he was panicking. He couldn't lose his little girl to that witch. "My ex-wife came back last night—to take Beth away with her. She's filed for custody."

Mac picked up the paper and looked at it. "You're right. I thought she didn't want children?"

"She didn't. She was furious when she got pregnant. And she asked Doc to tie her tubes. He asked me about it. I told him to do what she wanted. I certainly didn't care."

"So what changed her mind?"

"She said her husband wanted a child and she couldn't have any. She thought she'd take Beth since adoption took too long. Damn her!"

"Look, Ryan, I'm going to fight like hell to make sure she doesn't take your child away. First I'll make sure the custody hearing is held here. Then I'll prepare the case."

"Can you make it where she can't demand to see Beth? She couldn't even tell Beth and Mandy apart. She had the nerve to say it didn't matter. Either one of the girls would do. As if they were interchangeable!" Ryan jumped up and began pacing the office.

"How's Suzanne dealing with this?"

"She said she felt sorry for her that she couldn't have a baby. Ridiculous!"

"It's a good thing you and Suzanne married. We can prove that you have a good home life for Beth. Er, did you and Suzanne work out your problems?"

"Not yet, but we're getting along well."

"You'll probably have to endure a visit, or several visits from a state-appointed welfare worker. It would be important that you and Suzanne share a bedroom. That the kids think you share the same room."

Ryan froze, his body stiff. "What? Someone will come into my home? They'll want to see our sleeping arrangements?"

"Ryan, that's how they do these things. She makes a report to the judge."

"I'll take care of it," he said firmly. "It's important?" he asked again.

"Extremely important. I know the two of you are

providing a good home, but we want everything looking good.''

''Yes. When will they come?''

''I don't know. I do have an appointment in fifteen minutes. But we need to set up a day so that I can ask you questions about your marriage. And you say Doc treated her when she had Beth?''

''Yeah.''

''I'll take a statement from him, too.''

''Anything else?''

''Don't worry. The judge would have to be blind and deaf to choose her as a parent over you and Suzanne.''

''Thanks, Mac.''

''Take care of that little problem, okay?''

''Yeah, I will.'' Ryan walked out of the office, refusing to think about what he was going to have to do. But he'd do anything to keep his little girl.

Chapter Nine

Suzanne spent the morning fearing Tiffany might turn up again and worrying about what Mac would say. She tried not to let her agitation show, but Josh seemed to be watching her closely.

Finally, he came to stand beside her while the girls were finishing their coloring. "Is anything wrong?" he whispered.

"Why, no, Josh. Why would you ask that?"

"You're acting a little nervous."

"I guess I'm worried about that woman who came last night. I didn't like her."

"Neither did I. Was she Beth's mommy?"

Suzanne hesitated, then she said, "Yes, she was. But she left when Beth was a little baby because she didn't want to be a mommy."

"That's bad."

"Yes, it is." She stood. "I'm going to start making lunch."

"What are we having?"

"The meat loaf I made for dinner last night. Only we're going to make sandwiches. I'll fix a tray of fresh vegetables to go with it. Carrots, cucumbers, broccoli and cauliflower.''

"Okay.''

She knew Josh wouldn't be excited about vegetables, but she wanted to get the conversation on more mundane matters. Normal things. She didn't want to discuss the surreal events of last night. Tiffany's visit had even invaded her dreams.

She was working at the sink, cleaning the veggies when they heard a vehicle approach the house. Suzanne stared out the window over the sink and then breathed a sigh of relief when she saw Ryan's truck. "Ryan's back,'' she told the children.

They all left their seats at the table and ran out onto the porch to greet him.

She envied them their freedom. As an adult, she felt she had to maintain decorum, so she continued her work. But she felt a real sense of relief now that he was here. She no longer had to play guard dog. Ryan was home and he would protect them from Tiffany.

"Hi,'' she said as he entered the house with all three children hanging on him. "How did everything go?''

"Good,'' was his only response. It didn't satisfy her for a minute, but she knew it was all she'd get until the children went down for their nap.

"I see. Well, lunch is almost ready. Why don't you go wash up? Kids, you'd better wash your hands too.''

She put a slice of meat loaf and two pieces of bread on each plate. Then she put the big tray of fresh vegetables and dip on the table and added mustard, mayonnaise and ketchup.

"Hey, that looks good. But I may have to have two sandwiches," Ryan said as he came back into the kitchen. The children weren't as appreciative.

"I want potato chips," Beth said firmly.

"Me, too." Mandy agreed.

"No. The vegetables are better for you. They'll make you grow."

Suzanne was surprised when Ryan seconded her. "Susie is being a good mom, serving us the right kind of meals. We'll eat vegetables, just like she wants."

"Thanks."

He smiled at her. It wasn't the easy smile she'd grown to count on, still, it was a smile.

They all ate, though the girls, of course, couldn't finish their sandwiches. They discovered the joy of dipping the vegetables in dip. It made them eat a few more vegetables than they'd planned. Josh, too, had fun dipping.

Suzanne served them banana pudding for dessert. She'd used fat-free pudding. But she didn't tell them that secret, so everyone enjoyed it.

"Okay, its quiet time," she announced with a smile. The children all protested, but she ushered them from the room, knowing that Ryan wouldn't fill her in on his morning meeting with Mac until after the kids were safely out of hearing.

When she came back into the kitchen, Ryan had made a second sandwich and was finishing it off.

"You really were hungry," she exclaimed.

"This morning's work was a lot harder than chasing cows," he assured her.

"So, tell me what happened."

He looked down the long hallway. Seeing it empty, he said, "The kids are all in their rooms?"

"Yes. Mac didn't say you'd have to give up Beth, did he?" she asked, anguish in her voice.

"No, not exactly."

"Don't make me guess, Ryan!" she snapped in exasperation.

"He said it was a good thing I had married you, or I might not have a chance. Now I'm providing a good home. When the social services woman comes to evaluate our home life, everything will be hunky-dory if—" He stopped and Suzanne was ready to choke him.

"If what?"

"If we are man and wife."

"We have the license to prove it," she said, not quite understanding what he meant.

"But we don't share the same bedroom."

She stared at him, everything suddenly crystal-clear. "Why would that make a difference? We'll tell her you snore too loudly."

"No, I don't. And she'll ask the children why we don't sleep together and upset them. Susie, I know I said you could have time, but it just ran out. I can't risk losing Beth to that excuse for a mother. Not just for me. Beth would be miserable the rest of her life if she went to live with her mother."

"I know, I know."

"So, I'm asking you to sleep in my room. I'll

give you all the space you want. I'll even sleep on the floor, but—you've got to move in there.''

Suzanne nodded and whispered yes.

He stared at her. ''Just like that? You'll do it?''

''Yes,'' she nodded and calmly said. ''Yes, of course.''

He seized her by the shoulders and embraced her, tears in his eyes. ''Thank you.''

She eased herself from his embrace. ''We married for the children, Ryan. Of course I'll do what I have to do to keep them all safe.''

He drew a deep breath. ''We're going to have to act as if we're intimate around the kids, and we'll start right now, so they won't be surprised if I kiss you. Do you understand?''

''I'm not a child, Ryan. Of course I understand what you mean. I'll go move my things to your room while they're down for a nap.''

Ryan watched her go, her shoulders back, acting as if his request was normal.

He was grateful that she was trying to help him save his child. However, his life for the next month or two was going to be hell. He would have to pretend he was really married outside the bedroom. But in the bedroom, he would have to keep his distance. Some day, he'd explain to Beth how much he'd sacrificed for her...if it didn't drive him crazy in the meantime.

He stood and began clearing the table. Finally, he rinsed the dishes and put them in the dishwasher. Then he swept the kitchen floor.

Suzanne came back in and stared at him. "I think this is even more impressive than cooking, Ryan."

"Just a gesture of gratitude. I need to get in the saddle and check in with my men."

"All right. Just one more thing. Did you see Tiffany this morning when you were in town?"

"No, but I talked to some people who saw her last night. After she left here, she filled up her car at the station on the highway. She told Jimmy Boyd, who was working as cashier, she was going back to Dallas. She couldn't stand waiting in Cactus for no good reason."

Suzanne breathed a sigh of relief. "Good. I had nightmares about her sneaking in at night and stealing one of the girls."

He couldn't resist. He pulled her into his arms. "I'm sorry you're having to go through this, Suzanne. You're taking it like a good sport."

"You may change your mind about that if this situation goes on for a long time."

"I don't think so," he assured her. Then he dropped a kiss on her lips and left the house. He was going to be doing a lot of quick exits, he figured.

SUZANNE GREW more nervous as the afternoon passed and bedtime drew closer. She'd grown more confident of Ryan keeping his hands to himself as he'd understood her need for time. In fact, lately she'd grown more and more interested in the physical side of marriage.

Now that she would share his room…and his bed,

would it make them draw closer? She thought it might put more distance between them. She hoped not but...

"I can't?" Josh asked in surprise.

She snapped back to the present. "Can't what?"

"I wanted to draw a picture of the baby horse instead of coloring something today. Isn't that all right?"

"I think that's a wonderful idea, Josh. You have good drawing ability. I'm sorry. I was thinking about something else."

He accepted her explanation and took a clean sheet of paper. He really did have exceptional drawing ability for a four-year-old. Of course, he was very mature for his age, too. She supposed tragedy did that to kids. Mandy didn't seem to have been hurt by it, but she was still so very young.

Beth had been abandoned by her mother at such an early age, she didn't miss what she hadn't known. Gradually, however, she was getting used to having a female influence. She was particularly fond of having her nails painted.

Suzanne studied the two little girls. They both wore bangs that almost covered their eyes. Should she trim them herself, or make an appointment at the local beauty shop? She wanted the girls to learn that taking care of themselves was important. She'd seen friends who were afraid to spend a penny on themselves because their husbands wouldn't like it. Then their husbands left them because they looked old and worn out.

She picked up the phone and made an appointment for the four of them; Josh needed a trim, too. She'd talked herself into it without consulting Ryan. She could use her own money if necessary.

She laughed at herself. Ryan hadn't objected to anything she'd done. When they'd gone grocery shopping last weekend, she'd bought several unnecessary things she'd known the children would enjoy. He'd cheerfully paid the bill.

When he came in for dinner, it was almost ready and the children had washed their hands. Josh was waiting to show him the picture he'd made of the new colt they'd visited in the barn a couple of weeks ago. So, of course, the two little girls had to show him their drawings.

But there was a change in routine. He didn't greet the children first. He crossed the kitchen and turned Suzanne around and kissed her. ''I missed you,'' he whispered.

She turned a bright red. He was playacting for the children's sake, of course, but it was delightful, even knowing he didn't mean it.

All three children stared at them, but Mandy recovered first. ''Me, too!''

He turned from Suzanne and greeted the children. He went to wash up, promising to look at their efforts as soon as he returned.

Suzanne finished up dinner, but her hands were shaking. This physical stuff was more effective than she'd realized.

She waited with almost as much impatience as Josh for Ryan to see his work. Would he dismiss it because he thought being an artist was sissy work? Many men would.

Ryan came back in and sat down at the table. Then he asked Mandy to bring her picture to him. She proudly scooted down from the table and carried her paper to show him. She'd colored a picture of two chickens. The fact that one of them was colored blue didn't bother Ryan. He praised her work.

Then it was Beth's turn. She'd colored several trees green and a car black. Beth was very much the realist. Ryan praised her work too, telling her he was particularly fond of black cars.

That pleased Beth a lot.

Now it was Josh's turn. Suddenly, he didn't want to show Ryan his work. Ryan shot Suzanne a look, wondering what was going on. Suzanne stepped over to Josh's chair. "Honey, I think Ryan will like your work." She turned to Ryan. "You see, Josh drew his picture himself before he colored it."

"Well, of course I want to see it," Ryan said, smiling at the boy. With that encouragement, Josh put his drawing in front of Ryan.

For a moment, Ryan said nothing. Suzanne could understand his astonishment. Then he looked at Josh. "Son, this is so good. It looks just like the colt we saw. You did a great job." He hugged Josh and the boy beamed at him. Suddenly, he was talking about the drawing and how much he'd enjoyed making it. He even explained his debate about what the colt should be doing.

Suzanne finally had to interrupt him for them to have prayer so they could eat before the food got cold. Josh blushed at her gentle reprimand. But when the prayer was over, he continued talking about his work.

She'd promised the kids they could watch a Disney movie after dinner. When they'd finished eating, they asked to be excused, as she'd been teaching them to do. Ryan granted permission. Then they asked Suzanne to set up the movie.

Suzanne helped them settle in the den and started the movie, telling them she'd be in the kitchen, cleaning up after dinner.

She came back into the kitchen to discover Ryan had already begun clearing the table. "You've worked all day, Ryan. I can do these dishes."

"And you haven't worked all day? We'll do them together."

She stopped protesting. They worked side by side. Ryan said nothing at first. Then he asked, "Am I mistaken or is Josh showing a lot of talent in his drawing?"

"Yes, he is. I was thinking about finding someone to give him lessons. I've heard the art teacher at the high school did that occasionally."

"You don't think he's too young?"

"I'm not sure, but I can ask her. She lives here year-round."

"Okay. Will you have time to take him? If not, I can take off work."

"No, I can probably shop with the girls while he takes lessons. The girls will think they're getting a special treat, and Josh will be excited."

"You are amazing," he said, smiling at her and putting his arms around her waist.

"There's—there's no one around," she whispered, unnerved by his touch. She regretted her words at once. Ryan stiffened and frowned. Then he stepped away from her.

"I'd better go get caught up on my paperwork." He stalked out of the room, his feelings clearly hurt.

But how was she going to endure his touch, sleeping in the same bed with him, and then go back to just being friends when the custody battle was over? She really didn't know.

After the children were tucked in, she knocked on Ryan's study door and opened it. "The children are waiting for you to say goodnight."

He got up at once and went past her as she stood in the doorway. "Thanks."

She'd already cleaned the kitchen and prepared her list for the next day. She always planned her meals the night before. But she'd also done that chore. It was amazing how much time she had if Ryan didn't participate in the evening.

She went into the den to see what was on television, hoping Ryan would join her. But she heard him go back into his office and close the door. She slumped down on the cushions.

After half an hour of pretending to watch television, she turned it off and went to their bedroom. Just referring to it as "their" bedroom reminded her that her life was going to change, one way or another. She nervously entered the big room. What if he'd gone to bed and she hadn't noticed?

That was a joke. She'd been listening intently all evening. She got ready for bed, dressing in an opaque floor-length gown and robe. Then she stared at the king-size bed. There was no reason for Ryan to sleep on the floor. There was plenty of room for both of them with lots of room left in between.

She came out of the bedroom and moved to his office door. She drew a deep breath and knocked softly.

"Come in."

There was no welcome in his words. Only politeness. "I'm going to bed now."

"Good night." He kept his gaze on his desk.

"Ryan, I'm sorry I upset you earlier. It will take me some time to get used to—everything."

"Of course."

His voice was still cold.

"I wanted to tell you that I think there's plenty of room in the bed for both of us. You don't need to sleep on the floor."

"That's very kind of you, but I don't think so."

"Ryan!" she exclaimed, becoming impatient with his sulking. "I'm trying to be nice. But if you want to sleep on the floor, feel free to do so. I'm not going to try to stop you from being a martyr!" She left his office, and closed the door behind her with a snap.

Back in the big bedroom, she stood for a while, feeling a little lost. Her belongings seemed to have been absorbed by his. She didn't feel as though she had any part of the room. Slowly, she approached the bed and turned down the cover to the fresh sheets she'd put on the bed earlier that day.

Then she went into the bathroom to prepare for bed.

When she came out, she looked for Ryan. He still hadn't come. He'd probably spend the entire night in his office. Well, fine! She'd get a good night's sleep because this mattress was a lot better than that on the daybed she'd been sleeping on.

Suddenly she realized she didn't know which side of the bed he slept on. She debated going back to ask him, but then she made up her mind. She would be the first up, so she'd take the side closest to the door. That was where she'd plugged in her alarm clock. She left the bathroom light on and almost closed that door. Then she slid beneath the covers and settled in to go to sleep.

She figured she wouldn't really fall asleep until he came to bed. But she was wrong. Comfort and warmth soothed her troubled soul and she fell asleep.

RYAN HADN'T ACCOMPLISHED much in his office. Mostly he'd listened to Suzanne's movements about the house. He was glad she'd invited him to tell the children goodnight. It made him feel a part of the family, at least.

Now it was way past bedtime. But he was afraid to go into his own bedroom. Not until he was sure Suzanne was asleep. What if she was waiting up for him? If that was true, then all he was doing was causing them both to lose sleep.

He stood and crossed to the door, turning off the office light. After a deep breath, he went next door to his—their bedroom. He started to knock. Then he reached for the knob. It was still his room, too. He didn't have to knock.

The first thing he saw was Suzanne in his bed, sleeping on the side he always occupied. The light was dim, coming from the bathroom. But he could clearly see her outline in the bed. She was sound asleep.

He crossed to the bathroom and prepared for bed. When he came out, he snapped off the bathroom light and made his way to the other side of the bed. He slowly slid under the covers, trying not to awaken her. Apparently she was a sound sleeper, because she never moved.

Once he was stretched out, his head on his pillow, he took stock of his situation. He wasn't alone. His wife was sharing his bed. It wasn't exactly what he'd hoped for, but it would help him keep his daughter.

He reached over and found warm, soft skin. He instinctively turned toward her. He wasn't alone anymore.

Chapter Ten

When the alarm went off the next morning, Suzanne reached to turn it off, then she changed her movement to hit the snooze alarm. She felt particularly snug in her bed this morning. All warm and comfy.

Suddenly she realized why. Ryan's long arms held her against him. His body heat warmed her, too. She was thankful that he hadn't moved. She slowly eased away from his hold and got out of the bed, then she changed her alarm from Snooze to Off. The last thing she wanted was to wake Ryan up. She hoped he would sleep until after she was dressed.

She gathered her clothes and hurried to the bathroom. In five minutes, she had on her jeans and T-shirt and tennis shoes. She tied her hair back with a matching scarf and came back into the bedroom. She stopped by the bed.

"Ryan, I'm going to fix breakfast. You'd better wake up."

She hurried out the door, not bothering to wait for a response.

Ryan sat up in bed, staring as the door closed.

He'd been awake for a few minutes before the alarm went off. When daylight had crept into his bedroom, he'd awakened.

He'd discovered he was holding Suzanne against his body and he liked the feel of her. He didn't want to hurry out of bed. He hadn't slept this well in years. Tiffany hadn't been a snuggler.

He smiled, enjoying the feelings, before he finally crawled out of bed. He'd enjoyed sleeping with Suzanne. And if he went to bed after she went to sleep, he could repeat the experience every night.

When he reached the kitchen, she was cooking bacon. When the microwave beeped, he turned around, wondering if she'd cooked his eggs in the microwave as punishment. However, he discovered she'd made oatmeal in it, to serve with bacon and buttered toast.

"This is different," he said as he sat down in his chair and picked up his coffee cup.

"Don't you like oatmeal? I read that it's good for you. I won't fix it every day, but I thought it made a nice alternative."

"You're right, and I like it, if we have raisins."

"We do." She set a bowl of raisins on the table.

"You think of everything. And I like the fact that you worry about my health," he added with a grin. "It tells me you're not plotting my early demise."

His ridiculous statement, accusing her of trying to murder him, brought a smile to her full lips. He mentally chalked up a score for the good guys. He loved watching Suzanne smile. "Are the kids getting oatmeal, too?"

"Yes. It will be a good breakfast for when Josh starts school in the fall."

"He's going to go to school every day in September?"

"Yes, of course. He'll be pre-kindergarten, so he'll come home at noon. He can already count and do basic addition and subtraction, and he can read a little bit."

"Due to your good teaching."

"Actually," she said with a sad smile, "Mary Lee started teaching him. I've only carried on her work."

"That's a good thing to tell him when he's older and can appreciate his mother's care," Ryan said. "But I'm sorry I made you sad."

"No, I'm fine."

"Aren't you going to eat?"

She nodded and sat down with her own bowl of oatmeal. She'd started eating with him because otherwise he'd have to eat alone. The children had each other. Now she wished she hadn't. She didn't want to have any discussions about their sleeping arrangements. She didn't want to take a stand against him touching her during the night. It felt too good.

"So where will you be working today?" she asked.

"Several different places. But you can reach me on the cell phone if you need anything, right?"

"Yes, I guess I forgot."

"What do you have planned for today?"

"Oh, I didn't tell you. I'm taking the children in to town to get their hair trimmed. Beth and Mandy's bangs are almost covering their eyes and Josh's hair is getting too long.''

''My barber is Lionel. You can take Josh there.''

''I thought I'd get his hair trimmed in the beauty shop.''

''Absolutely not,'' Ryan said firmly. ''He'd be embarrassed if any of the boys saw him. It's bad enough that he has to go in there at all. They'll call him a sissy.''

''That's ridiculous. I'm sure lots of little boys get their hair done in the beauty shop. They certainly did in Dallas,'' she protested, now determined to have Josh's hair cut there.

''We don't do things the same as city folks. Take him to Lionel.''

She heard the children getting up and immediately jumped to her feet to prepare their oatmeal. There was plenty of bacon cooked. She popped in toast to brown, too.

Josh came in, rubbing his eyes. ''Morning,'' he said to Ryan.

Suzanne knew from experience that he didn't wake up fast. ''Here's some chocolate milk for you, sweetie.'' That got his attention. She hadn't given them chocolate milk for breakfast. He grabbed the glass and took a long drink.

''Hey, that's real good,'' he said, waking up a little.

''Yeah,'' Ryan agreed. ''Why didn't I get any?'' he asked, as if he were one of the children.

Suzanne ignored him.

The two male figures were whispering as the little

girls came to the table. Then, Josh asked if Ryan could have some chocolate milk.

She knew Ryan had put him up to asking. "After I pour the girls some."

"Some what?" Beth asked with a yawn.

"Chocolate milk," Josh informed her, "and it's really good."

She'd offered the children the chocolate milk as a reward for eating oatmeal to make sure the new breakfast went over well. It wasn't necessary to bribe Ryan. But she poured him a big glass of the chocolate milk. He grabbed her arm as she set the glass on the table.

Pulling her closer, he kissed her on the lips. "Thanks, honey," he said, smiling at her.

The two girls were tasting the milk and ignored the byplay. But Josh grinned at her, seemingly pleased.

"What's this?" Beth asked, moving the spoon in her cereal a little.

"It's oatmeal," Suzanne said firmly, "and it goes with the chocolate milk. Look, you can put raisins in it too, like Dad did."

After Ryan said the cereal was so good that he wanted some more, the girls ate theirs, too. She supposed she should be grateful that Ryan's actions entertained the children. When he got up to leave, he apologized for not having time to help with the dishes, but he told her each of the children would carry their dishes to the sink.

He kissed her goodbye while the children

watched, and she couldn't say anything. Oh, my, this playacting was delicious and difficult, all at the same time.

SHE LOADED UP the children in her car and drove into town so they could get there in time for their appointment.

She couldn't quite bring herself to ignore Ryan's warning, so she offered Josh the option of having his hair cut at the barber shop like Ryan did. Josh immediately breathed a sigh of relief.

"Thank you, Susie. I was really worried."

"Why didn't you tell me? I thought we were going to talk if something bothered you?" she asked, unhappy that she'd almost upset him.

"It's not that big a deal, but I like the idea of going to the barber shop."

"Okay, fine."

"I want to go to the barber shop, too," Beth insisted.

Suzanne should've expected that. "No, you go to the girls' barber shop. It's called a salon. They even polish your nails there."

"I get my nails polished today?" Beth squealed.

Suzanne had made a mistake, she knew, because Mandy, of course, demanded she have her nails done, too. This was going to be one heck of an expensive outing.

After an hour at the salon, they were finally through. They left the salon and crossed the square to the barber shop. Josh's hair was quickly cut and Suzanne was herding them back to the car when she heard someone call her name.

She turned around and discovered Jessica on the steps of her restaurant, waving them over. "What are you doing in town this morning?" she asked.

Immediately the girls extended their hands, palms down to her.

"It was haircut day for all of us, so we added in a manicure for the girls."

"Sam says Cassie loves to get her nails done."

"Well, that makes me feel better. I spent a lot of money because I had to convince the girls they should go to the salon instead of the barber shop."

Jessica laughed. "I understand the problem. I tried to get the boys to the salon to get their hair cut and they threw a fit. They said it was too girly."

"Thanks, I'm glad to hear other people have the same problems."

"Come on in the restaurant and have lunch. Then we can really visit. I heard about you-know-who coming back."

Suzanne looked at the children. It would be a relief to talk about her concerns with someone other than Ryan. And Jessica had proven to be a friend.

"The children—"

"Why don't we take them to Mabel's house? She's baby-sitting mine today. I'll have some hamburgers made up and they can all eat their lunch together while we enjoy some freedom."

"Would she mind? That would be wonderful. I haven't had any time off since the wedding."

"I know. But Ryan praises you to the skies with everyone he talks to."

Suzanne's cheeks turned red.

"While I'm getting the food, come in and call Melanie and see if she can join us. Then call Alex. Sam is working today so she can't come."

"What a great idea. Thank you so much, Jessica."

She felt a little guilty about her decision, but she knew Ryan could eat with the men. She called home first and left a message on the machine so he wouldn't worry. Then she called Melanie and Alex. They both said they'd be there in fifteen minutes.

When the children learned they would get to play with Cal and Jessica's two boys, they were excited. When she got back to the restaurant after dropping them off, Suzanne said, "I've been trying to meet their every need, but I've realized today they need to interact with other children."

"Right. We should've told you about Mother's Day Out at the church. It's on Tuesdays and Thursdays from ten to three. They supervise the children, teaching them how to play nicely with others. It helps prepare them for school. You have to bring a lunch for each child and then they have pallets and they sleep until three."

"Oh, that would be wonderful! I'll have to talk to Ryan about it, but I don't think he'd object."

"He shouldn't," Melanie added as she slid into the booth. "It keeps all of us sane."

Alex joined them. "What are you talking about?"

"How Mother's Day Out saves us. If you only talk to little children, you start treating even your husband as a small child. Sometimes, I actually use the time to go to a movie," Melanie confessed.

Suzanne stared at her. "You have time to see a movie?"

"The church ladies planned the hours so you can see a movie that lets out at two-forty five. It's perfect."

"Oh, mercy, how wonderful!"

They chatted all through their lunch and didn't discuss Tiffany until they'd finished. Then Alex said, "Did you see Tiffany when she came to the ranch?"

"Yes, we were having dinner when she walked in on us."

"Typical. She never had any manners. She did what she wanted no matter who it hurt," Alex huffed.

"Do you know, she asked which one was Beth? She couldn't recognize her own child."

"Does Mac know that?"

"I don't know. She said it didn't matter which girl she took as long as she got one. She said she couldn't have children. I was feeling sorry for her until Ryan told me she insisted on having her tubes tied because she never wanted to get pregnant again." Suzanne knew she sounded indignant, but she couldn't help it.

Alex looked thoughtful. "I'll talk to Samantha as well as Doc. They might be able to reverse the sterilization process. I believe they're having some luck with that kind of surgery these days."

Suzanne stared at Alex and burst out laughing. "Oh, I'd love to be there when you tell Tiffany that."

"You probably will be," Alex said, grinning in return. "I suspect Mac would save that information until they're in the courtroom. Her reaction might prompt the truth."

Suzanne felt much better when they finished. Melanie went with her to Mother's Day Out to sign her children up at once. The teachers gave her a list of rules and told her they'd be happy to have her children.

She drove home, listening to the chatter of the children about their afternoon. They all seemed to have had a good time. Beth in particular, being an only child, had been staying with Ryan's cousin all alone. Suzanne felt Mother's Day Out was going to be a really good experience for Beth.

She gave the children some activities to do while she hurriedly began fixing dinner. When Ryan came in at six, she had everything ready, as usual. But he didn't smile, and he didn't give her a kiss, even though the children were there.

"Ryan? Is something wrong?"

"You dumped the kids the first chance you got? I thought you liked being a mom."

Suzanne took a step back, unhappy with his words.

"Yeah, Dad," Josh said, not realizing the way the wind was blowing. "We got to play with some other kids and have real hamburgers. It was fun."

Immediately the two girls wanted to add their stories.

She listened to their happy chatter, but she turned her back on Ryan. Putting everything on the table, she told the children to sit in their chairs. She didn't say anything to Ryan.

"I have to go wash my hands," he announced.

She nodded but still didn't talk to him. She hadn't told him she'd signed the children up for Mother's Day Out all summer. She could tell he'd be against it. Could she keep it a secret from him?

No, she wouldn't go down that road. She'd try to persuade him.

He joined them at the table. She had the children bow their heads for the blessing. Then she began passing the bowls around the table, helping Mandy, who sat beside her.

The children continued to talk. She knew Ryan couldn't fail to see their enjoyment. However, after he'd begun to relax, he stiffened when Josh informed him that they were going to go play with other children every Tuesday and Thursday.

She said nothing but stared at Ryan as he turned to face her.

After a moment, he said, "We'll talk about this after dinner."

"Fine." She'd hardly eaten anything, but she put down her fork and took her plate to the sink. Then she took the children's plates as they finished. Ryan continued to eat, but he watched her every move.

Josh sensed for the first time that everything wasn't well. "What will you talk about?" he asked cautiously.

Suzanne answered him before Ryan could. "Adult things, sweetie. Don't worry about it. Want to make a drawing this evening since you didn't get to draw this morning? Oh, did you ask Dad if he liked your haircut?''

"I suppose you took him to the salon?" Ryan asked, his voice bitter.

She said nothing.

"No, Dad. She asked me where I wanted my hair to be cut. I said I wanted to go to the barber. So I went to Mr. Lionel."

"And we got our nails painted," the little girls remembered. They stuck their fingers out for him to admire.

He did so, pleasing all three children. While they talked, Suzanne fixed ice cream for the four of them. She wasn't interested in sitting at the table and trying to eat. She might throw up if she did.

"Didn't have time to bake anything?" Ryan suddenly asked. Her anger got the best of her. She picked up his ice cream and dumped it in the sink. Then she walked out of the kitchen in the utter silence that had fallen.

She heard Ryan say something to the children that made them laugh. She was glad he felt happy. She didn't. Things had been going so well. But suddenly it had fallen apart because she wanted a little time without the children.

She would've blamed herself if her friends weren't doing the same thing with their husbands' approval. That made her feel like her idea might not be quite as ridiculous as Ryan seemed to think it was.

She couldn't go to the bedroom and shut him out. So she returned to the little room she'd slept in until last night. She closed the door and sat on the little bed. She'd forgotten to bring in a magazine or something to occupy her time. But she wasn't going to take care of the children tonight. Ryan could enjoy that duty.

THE KIDS WERE UNEASY about everything with Suzanne not around.

"I think she has a headache," Ryan told them, unable to come up with another reason…unless he told them the truth, and he didn't think that was a good idea.

Obviously the children hadn't suffered from their outing, but twice a week? Wouldn't it look like she didn't want to be a mother? It had taken Ryan by surprise, making him think maybe she was going to turn into another Tiffany. But he'd obviously jumped to the wrong conclusion.

He should've taken time to think about things. Suzanne had been wonderful from the minute he'd insisted they marry. But she did have a temper. He remembered she'd confessed she'd lost her temper when she'd fired the cowboys who'd been stealing from the kids.

Tonight, when he'd asked that ridiculous question, she'd lost it again and thrown out his bowl of ice cream. He'd joked with the kids that she was putting him on a diet. They'd laughed a little, but they'd also watched him carefully.

"Well, were you going to do some drawing, Josh? We'll get the table cleaned off, and then you can draw in here. What do you want to draw?"

"I want to draw a cowboy," Josh said slowly, considering his choice.

"Good idea. Girls, what are you going to color?"

"Susie helps us choose," Beth told him.

"How about I help you choose tonight? We'll let Susie have the night off." It suddenly occurred to him that she never had the night off. He talked to the kids and admired their work, but she always had activities for them after dinner. She performed mommy duties until the children went to bed.

He stayed in the kitchen with the children and watched them do their coloring and drawing. He'd cleaned the kitchen, too. He wasn't sure where Suzanne was. She hadn't left the house by the back door, but she could've slipped out the front door.

He was anxious to talk to her. He had to explain that he'd jumped to conclusions. That he was afraid it would look bad to the judge.

The phone rang and he answered. "Hello?"

"Ryan, this is Spence."

Ryan greeted him, wondering why he'd called.

"We're going to start up our family rodeos next weekend. We wondered if you'd like to have the first one at your house. You can explain to Suzanne that it's potluck. Everyone brings food. She doesn't have to fix everything."

"Oh, yeah, that will be fun, Spence. I'm sure Suzanne will enjoy that. Let me call you tomorrow to let you know. I can't spring things like this on her without explaining."

"I know what you mean. But we heard you had the perfect animals for riding."

"You're right. I'll give you a call tomorrow."

Great. Now he had to apologize to Suzanne and tell her about the rodeo at the same time. Let's see, he could say "sorry about the reaction tonight. And by the way, I'm inviting about twelve families to dinner next weekend. You won't mind, will you, dear?"

Yeah, that'd work…not!

Chapter Eleven

He found Suzanne sleeping in her old bed, traces of tears on her cheeks.

He felt like a heel. Especially since he realized mothers never had any time off. It wasn't that he would object to her taking the children to Mother's Day Out. Not anymore. It was that he feared what the judge would think. He'd have to call Mac and ask him.

That was it. He'd call Mac.

He closed the door on Suzanne and headed for the phone in the kitchen.

"Mac? It's Ryan. I have a question that couldn't wait. I hope you don't mind."

"Of course not, Ryan. What's so important?"

"Would it make the judge think Suzanne isn't a good mother if she took the kids to Mother's Day Out?"

Mac didn't respond at once and fear grew in Ryan.

"Why would you think that?"

''Because she's dumping them off on someone else, like she wasn't happy about being a mother.''

Mac heaved a big sigh. ''Ryan, you've got a lot to learn. And you took care of Beth by yourself all that time? Did you notice that you had no time for yourself once you picked up Beth until she went to bed?''

''Well, yeah, but I had work to do at night.''

''Did you think Suzanne was going to lie on a chaise lounge and eat chocolates while the children were at Mother's Day Out?''

''No, of course not, but—''

''The judge knows mothering is a twenty-four-hour-a-day job. If a woman gets a break every once in a while, it keeps her happy. Besides, it's good for the kids. Josh is starting pre-K next year. He needs to learn to get along with children his own age. It will make going to school less traumatic. And Beth has been an only child until recently. She needs training on playing with groups of children. And Mandy will do better than either of them because she's starting early.''

''Wow! I didn't know you were a child expert.''

''I'm not, but my wife is.''

''So the judge won't hold it against Suzanne?''

''Of course not. Did Spence call you about Saturday?''

''Yes. But I didn't get a chance to talk to Suzanne about it tonight. We—had to discuss Mother's Day Out.''

''Don't tell me you told her she shouldn't do that.''

"Not exactly," Ryan said uneasily, rubbing the back of his neck. "I made a stupid remark about her not making dessert when she served us ice cream. She lost her temper and threw my ice cream in the sink."

Mac laughed. "Cal said you were dumber than rocks. You're lucky she didn't take your head off. I hope you're ready to apologize."

"Yeah, I'm ready. But I'm not sure I can apologize and spring the rodeo thing on her in the same breath."

"Want us to have it at Spence's?"

"No. I really want to have it here. I've got a couple of bulls I've really wanted someone to try. I'll talk to her about it tomorrow."

He got off the phone and returned to the little room where Suzanne was sleeping. Gently, he scooped her into his arms and carried her to his big bed. He got a washcloth and wet it. Then he wiped her face clear of the tears she'd shed. She came awake.

"What are you doing?" she asked, her voice still drowsy.

"Wiping away your tears. I'm sorry I made you cry."

She abruptly sat up. "What am I doing in here?"

"Remember? You promised to sleep in here so the judge would think we were happily married."

"I don't think I'm that good an actress!"

He winced. She was definitely still angry. "Sweetheart, I know I was wrong. But you took me by surprise and I thought you were like Tiffany, trying to get rid of the kids."

She opened her mouth, anger in her eyes, and he held up a hand to stop her. "I know, I know. Not only do you deserve some time for yourself, but it's good for the kids. Mac explained it all to me. But I was afraid the judge would hold it against us. I just couldn't risk losing Beth."

"And Mac said he wouldn't?"

"Yeah. I mean, no, he won't."

"So you're satisfied that I'm not hurting Beth's chances to stay here?"

"Yeah. I knew better if I'd just stopped to think. But I didn't. Think, that is."

"I'm sorry I threw out your ice cream. I lost my temper."

"It's that red hair. I told the kids you were putting me on a diet," he explained.

"That's not what you need. I need to fatten you up a little."

Her smile filled him with relief. She'd forgiven him. "Thank you, Susie for forgiving me. Mac said husbands had to apologize a lot, and clearly he's right."

"You're a wonderful daddy, Ryan. I didn't explain it correctly."

Now he felt really bad. She was apologizing to him. He decided to get past everything tonight. "Look, Spence, Melanie's husband, called tonight. Every spring, we have some Saturday rodeos. It's potluck. The ladies all visit while we rodeo. Then we have dinner outside. It's a fun thing to do and it helps the guys with rodeo dreams in their heads to get a more realistic picture of their chances.''

"How wonderful. Will we be invited?" Suzanne asked, her eyes wide.

Ryan groaned.

"What's wrong? Won't they invite us?"

"Honey, they not only invited us, they want us to host the first one."

Her eyes were still wide, but he didn't think she'd quite taken it all in. He hurriedly added, "You just have to make gallons of iced tea. They'll all bring food. We'll set up some picnic tables and buy paper plates and cups."

"They want us to have the rodeo here?" she asked. Her voice was still disbelieving.

"Well, see, I've got some bulls that I think would make good rodeo bulls. But I'm not sure. If they perform well, I can sell them to a company that supplies bulls to the rodeo. Otherwise, they'll be hamburger meat. So—"

"Oh, good heavens, of course we'll host. Don't tell me some bull's life depends on me making iced tea! That—that's barbaric!"

He put his hands on her shoulders, gently calming her, the way he'd settle down a horse. "Now don't get upset, honey. That's how life is on a ranch. It's no big deal."

She shuddered.

He got back to the subject. "So, it's all right with you?" he asked, hesitantly.

"You didn't tell Spence yes?"

"No, I wanted to talk to you about it first."

She ducked her head. "I'm sorry. I hope that didn't embarrass you."

"No, not at all. Now, why don't you put on your pj's and get to sleep. The alarm rings early in the morning."

"But I didn't clean the kitchen!" She exclaimed, remembering the evening.

"The kids and I did it. Not as well as you might have, but the dishes are in the dishwasher and I swept the floor while the kids worked on their drawings."

"Thank you, Ryan." Then, for the first time, she leaned over and kissed his cheek. She'd received his kisses often enough, but she'd never offered him one, not even on the cheek.

He drew back hurriedly because his first inclination was to grab her and roll across the bed with her in his arms, kissing as they went.

"Uh, you take the bathroom first."

Her cheeks were red as she hurried to the chest of drawers, got out something to wear to bed and ducked into the bathroom, firmly closing the door behind her.

Lord have mercy, he was in trouble. She was such a sweet thing, apologizing to him when the fault was his. Agreeing to host the rodeo on such short notice. He'd gotten lucky with his marriage of convenience. He gave a silent prayer of thanks, and he also prayed he wouldn't screw it up. Suzanne was worth a long wait if necessary.

When she came out she was dressed in modestly fashioned pajamas made from a slinky blue material that his fingers ached to stroke. He got off the bed. "I'll—uh, I'll get ready for bed. Thanks again for putting up with my lack of understanding."

She smiled and he bolted into the bathroom. Lordy, he had to get better at resisting temptation.

He took a long time in the bathroom, hoping she would be asleep before he came out. Luck was on his side. He could hear her even breathing as he tiptoed to the bed. He got in and automatically reached for her as if he'd slept with her for years. Then he closed his eyes. Everything was right in his world again.

AT BREAKFAST the next morning, it was obvious the children were worried about what had happened the night before. Suzanne made a special effort to appear serene. Finally, when that didn't appear to soothe them, she said, "I'm sorry I lost my temper last night, kids. It was wrong of me. Dad and I talked things over last night and he forgave me."

"And she forgave me," Ryan hurriedly added. "It happens with married people, you know. Especially when the woman has red hair!" he added, a big grin on his face.

Josh laughed with relief. "Yeah, especially with Mom because of her red hair!"

All the children laughed, not even noticing that Josh had called her Mom instead of Susie.

Suzanne cleared her throat, not wanting any emotion to show. "Dad has another surprise for you, too."

"I do?" Ryan asked, surprised.

She gave him a disgusted look. "We're having the neighborhood rodeo here on Saturday. I think you'll enjoy it."

"Oh, yeah!" Josh said with enthusiasm. "We went to one last year with Dad and Mom. It was great, even though Mom got mad at Dad 'cause he rode a wild bull." He paused, a surprised look on his face. "Oh, I guess you're right. Married people do have arguments sometimes."

"Well, I don't blame your mama if she got upset with your dad. That's a dumb thing to do," Suzanne said cheerfully.

The sudden silence surprised her. She turned around and looked at the children, all of them staring at Ryan. His face had turned red.

"You wouldn't!" she snapped, staring at him.

"Hell, Susie, that's what you do at a rodeo."

"Watch your language, Mister! And don't think you're going to get away with that stupid excuse. 'All my friends are doing it' is not an intelligent reason."

"Um, I've got to go. We'll talk about it tonight." He jumped to his feet and kissed her cheek. Then he headed for the back door.

Suzanne was left holding the coffeepot, a frown on her face.

All morning, she worried about Ryan doing such a dumb thing. Then she decided to call Jessica to see if she had time for lunch on Thursday, the next day, when she took the children to Mother's Day Out.

"Oh, yes, I'm looking forward to it. We'll clue you in on the rodeo, too."

"I'm glad you brought that up. Do the men actually ride those angry bulls?"

"Well, they used to. Even Cal doesn't much anymore. He's afraid he's getting so old his bones will break." Jessica laughed.

"But don't they all take that risk? I know Ryan's a little younger, but it could happen to him."

"It could. But—what are you going to do? Their machismo is important to them. And Sam will be there in case they get hurt."

"Oh. And will Mac and Samantha come to the rodeo. A lawyer? Does Mac ride bulls, too?"

"Yeah. We'll talk tomorrow, Suzanne. It's not as bad as it sounds."

"Okay, I'll see you in the morning."

She hung up the phone, still worried, but feeling a little better than she had. At least she wouldn't worry alone.

With the children watching *Sesame Street,* she started a major cleaning of the already clean house. She couldn't have people thinking she wasn't a good housekeeper.

When Ryan came in that night, the house fairly glowed. "Wow, the house looks nice. You must've worked hard today."

"I did. That's why we're having hamburgers tonight. They're easy to fix."

He smiled at her. "One of my favorite meals. Did you kids help Mom clean?"

"A little," Josh said. "It wasn't a lot of fun."

"No, but it's necessary. You'd better learn now so a lady will be willing to marry you one day," Ryan said.

"Do you clean house?" Josh asked suspiciously.

"We did the dishes last night, didn't we, for Mom when she had a headache?"

He apparently struck a chord in Mandy's mind. "I help!" she announced with pride.

"You did, sweetheart. We all helped. We may not be as good as Mom, but we're all going to help."

After dinner, they all carried their plates to Suzanne, who rinsed them and put them in the dishwasher. The children began playing a game of Candyland and Ryan was supposed to help them, but he kept getting distracted by Suzanne moving about the kitchen.

"Uh, Susie, why did you work so hard on cleaning the house today?"

"Because the entire neighborhood will be here this weekend. I don't want them to think I'm a bad housekeeper."

"Dad! Mandy took four spaces and she only gets three," Josh protested.

"Uh, Josh is right, Mandy. Let's count to three," Ryan said. As soon as they'd corrected Mandy's mistake, he turned to Suzanne again. "That wasn't necessary. I told you it would be outside."

She gave him a droll look. "A lot you know. People will have to go to the bathroom and if it gets too hot, of course, we'll come inside to chat. The ladies will be in and out of the kitchen. There'll be food to store in the refrigerator or heat in the oven."

He frowned. "I hadn't—"

"Dad!" Josh protested again. "Beth is going the wrong way."

"Uh, right, Beth, you have to go up the mountain."

"But I don't want to slide down. If I go there I have to slide."

"That's the way the game works. You have to follow the rules."

"Always?" Beth asked.

He looked at Suzanne and said, "Always, sweetheart."

"Okay," Beth agreed in disgust. Then she added, "Your turn, Daddy."

Suzanne left the kitchen and his attention turned to the game.

"Okay." He'd be glad when the children got big enough for better games. Candyland didn't interest him much.

When they finished the game, Suzanne hadn't returned to the kitchen. He called her name and she came to the door.

"Have you finished? Good. It's bath time. Girls, I have your bath ready. And it has bubbles."

With shrieks of excitement, the girls ran after Suzanne.

"Girls!" Josh said with disgust. "I guess we have to put away the game."

"Yeah. I forgot to stop the girls. But it won't take much work to put the game away."

"Yeah, but it's not fair that Beth and Mandy don't have to help."

"Does Mom let you get away with that complaint?"

Josh looked offended. "No."

"That's what I thought. See? The game is already back in the box. Do you know where Mom keeps the games?"

"Yeah, over here on this shelf." Josh opened a cabinet and stacked the Candyland box on top of other games, then he came back to sit at the table. "Dad? Do you think Mom minds us calling her that?"

"No, not at all. Why?"

"Well, first we called her Susie 'cause our real mom called her that. But it's easier to call her Mom. When we played with those other kids, I had to explain why I called her Susie. And I didn't want to."

"I think Susie wants you to call her whatever you like. But I like it when you call me Dad."

"You do?"

"I do. We're going to have to get on with the horse-riding lessons, too. Tomorrow—oh, I guess you're going to Mother's Day Out. Well, then, Friday, we'll start our lessons. After lunch, when the girls take their nap, I'll take you with me."

"I don't think I'll be able to ride much at first," the boy said, a touch of fear in his eyes.

"No, of course not. I'll take you with me, sitting in front of me. And I'll hold on to you real tight. That will get you used to being in the saddle. When you're on a horse by yourself, you won't get out of the corral for a while, until you think you're ready."

"Oh. That sounds good. You'll hold on to me?"

"I promise."

"Okay," Josh said with a grin. "Wait until I tell the guys tomorrow."

"Tell them what, Josh?" Suzanne asked from the door.

"Dad's going to let me ride on his horse with him Friday afternoon. Isn't that neat?"

"Yes, it is. And he'll hold on to you real tight?"

"I promised," Ryan assured her, his lips curving up at the sight of the worry on her face. "I won't do anything dangerous, honey, I promise."

"I know. It's just that— He's only four."

"I'll be five in June, Mom. I gotta learn to ride a horse before I start school."

"I guess so. It's time for your bath. I rinsed away all the bubbles."

"Maybe Josh would like to take a shower. That's what most men do. How about it, Josh?" Ryan asked.

"Hey, yeah."

"Then your father will have to help you. Take your pajamas and clean underwear with you, so you don't get stranded with just a towel," she warned.

Josh leaped up and ran for his room.

"Thanks to your suggestion, you get to instruct Josh about showers, Ryan. Do a good job."

"Yes ma'am," he said giving her a mock salute as if she were a general.

It would also keep them from discussing him riding bulls on Saturday. He got a feeling that Suzanne didn't want to discuss it either. Why, he wondered?

He was discovering that marriage to Suzanne

wasn't as simple as he'd thought it would be. He'd thought in terms of meals, cleaning and occasional sex. He wasn't getting any sex, the meals were terrific and the house was cleaner than it had been since his mom died. But there was more going on every day than when just he and Beth had lived here. His life was richer, more fun. And they'd only been married a little over a month.

If he ever got to have sex, too, he couldn't imagine how wonderful life would be.

Chapter Twelve

When Suzanne met her friends on Thursday for lunch, she quietly listened to the latest gossip and to information about the rodeo and potluck dinner to be held on Saturday.

When conversation died a little, she asked the question that had been in her head since she'd learned about the rodeo.

"Does Ryan usually participate?"

Everyone stared at her. "What do you mean, participate?" Alex asked. "It's going to be on his ranch."

"Well, of course he'll participate as host, but does he—does he actually get on the back of one of these wild animals?"

"Depends on how many riders we've got," Jessica said, not looking at Suzanne. "Sometimes he does it three or four times."

Suzanne couldn't breathe. She gasped several times and Samantha, who had joined the group today, pounded her on her back. "Are you all right? Suzanne?"

"I'm—I'm fine. But I don't understand why he would do such a stupid thing." Her hands were shaking, and she still looked pale.

"Take it easy, Suzanne. Men are that way, you know, having to prove they're macho. Ryan is one of the best in the area. Some people think he could've won a national championship if he'd followed the rodeo," Jessica said.

"People would honestly recommend such a way of life?"

Alex laughed. "Just like they recommend playing pro football or baseball if the guy is lucky. He makes his money and retires, set for life."

"Surely they don't make that much in the rodeo," Suzanne protested.

"A few of them do. Rodeo riders also make money modeling and from advertisement deals. And Ryan is good-looking. He'd do well," Melanie said.

"Oh, mercy! What if he gets hurt?"

"I'm there," Samantha assured her. "I can fix broken bones."

"Yes, but I heard of a cowboy being killed at a professional rodeo last year. And on Saturday it won't be professional."

The other women said nothing. Finally, Samantha said, "That kind of accident is rare."

"As rare as a man and his wife being killed and leaving two children orphaned because an old man has a heart attack? And can you imagine how Josh and Mandy would react if their new daddy dies before their very eyes? How Beth would feel about it?"

She could feel herself getting hysterical, but she couldn't seem to help it. But if she didn't calm down, she'd blurt out how important Ryan had become to her. She would tell them how she would feel, now that she'd finally found a man she could trust enough to want to commit her life to him, if he died in front of her.

Samantha seemed to realize her difficulty. She calmly picked up a glass of ice water and told Suzanne to drink it slowly. Then she added to Jessica, ''Get a piece of Katie's carrot cake. She needs something sweet.''

Suzanne wanted to tell them it wasn't true. She was fine. But she knew she wasn't. There had been too much tragedy in her life. She didn't want any more. Not now. Not when she'd fallen in love with Ryan Walker…her husband.

Samantha was taking her pulse, and Melanie was saying soothing words to her, stroking her arm.

''I—I'm all right,'' she managed to get out, but everyone ignored her words, watching her shake, seeing her pale face and her shallow breathing. Jessica came back to the table with a piece of carrot cake. The Last Roundup was famous for its desserts from Katie's bakery.

Samantha put a fork in her hand. ''Suzanne, I want you to start eating the cake. You can have water if you want it to go with it, but don't stop eating until I tell you.'' Her words were firm, and Suzanne automatically followed her order.

Cal and Mac came into the restaurant and stopped

by the table where the ladies were gathered. Jessica got up and pulled the two men away.

Suzanne knew what they were going to do. They were going to tell Ryan he couldn't ride this weekend. But she couldn't allow that, as much as she didn't want him to do such a stupid thing. She couldn't shame him in front of his friends. "No! No, Jessica!" She pulled Jessica back and pleaded, "Don't—don't tell them."

"But then Ryan wouldn't ride this weekend."

"No. I can't ask that of him. He would be shamed in front of his friends. I'll manage. Please don't."

Jessica blew Cal a kiss and sent him and Mac to another table. "Are you sure, Suzanne? We're used to this stuff, but you've been through a lot of changes the past month and you're new to ranch life. Ryan would understand."

The other women nodded, but Suzanne saw the doubt in their eyes. "I'll hide in the house. As long as I don't see it," she whispered. "I shouldn't have let myself get upset. It was silly of me."

"Eat more cake," Samantha ordered.

Suzanne nodded and took another bite. "This is wonderful cake. Maybe I'll buy one for Saturday. Would that be okay?"

"It would be great," Alex said with a grin. "I'll have to go off my usual diet, of course."

Everyone laughed, a little louder than necessary, but they were glad a crisis had been averted.

"We didn't take you seriously at first, but we hadn't thought about the situation from your point of view, Suzanne. I still think someone should have a talk with Ryan. He's an intelligent man. But this is everyday stuff to him.''

"Yes, and it will become that to me. I have to adjust.''

"You're asking a lot of yourself,'' Melanie said softly.

"No, I'm fine. And since I learned about Mother's Day Out, I even have some time for myself. I appreciate you telling me about it.''

"Ryan didn't mind, did he?''

Suzanne closed her eyes as she felt her paleness replaced by redness. "Um, well, he thought the judge would hold it against me, and that I was turning into another Tiffany before his very eyes.''

Alex stared at her. "Why would the judge protest?''

"Ryan said it would look as though I don't want to be with the children. That I was tired of cooking and cleaning and taking care of the kids.''

"Men!'' Samantha said in disgust.

"It's all right. Mac told him it was a good thing, since you had educated him, Samantha.''

"Didn't you educate Ryan? I would have done so in several different languages for thinking I didn't need a break from twenty-four-hour duty.'' Alex said.

"Well, I did lose my temper,'' Suzanne said apologetically. "I really do have a temper.''

"Red hair,'' Jessica said. "My hair is really brown, but Cal teases me that it has red highlights. What did you do to Ryan?''

"I served the kids ice cream that night for dessert

and he asked me if I was too busy to make dessert.'' The women all looked outraged, which made Suzanne feel better. "So I took his ice cream and dumped it in the sink. Then I left him with the children the rest of the evening.''

They cheered.

"It was juvenile of me,'' Suzanne confessed.

"It was healthier than holding the resentment inside. And it didn't hurt anyone.'' Samantha said. Then she added, "I think it was brilliant.''

Suzanne sighed. "You all are such good friends. And thank you for humoring me during my hysteria. Um, what does one wear to the rodeo?''

"Jeans or shorts or a summer dress,'' Alex said. "Whatever's cool and comfortable.''

"I wear jeans because I might have to—I mean, some of the kids skin their knees and things, you know,'' Samantha said.

Suzanne knew she'd changed her reason because she really wore jeans in case she had to crawl into the arena and patch up a cowboy. But she wasn't going to think about that. And she would stay in the house while Ryan demonstrated his machismo.

At home that evening, they all gathered at the dinner table. She'd fixed a special meal, just in case it was one of Ryan's last meals. The children had had a good time at Mother's Day Out and Ryan patiently listened to their stories, one at a time. When they'd finished, he looked at Suzanne. "And what about your day? How did it go?''

"Fine.''

He'd been taking a bite of pie when she answered.

He frowned and looked at her, not eating the pie. "That's all? You have nothing to tell?"

"Um, no." She jumped up from her chair to take her dishes to the sink.

He didn't ask her again, but he watched her while they played Candyland with the children that evening. When Josh wanted to ask about Ryan riding the bulls on Saturday, Suzanne took the girls for their bubble bath. She was determined not to interfere with Ryan's life and embarrass him in front of his friends. But if she thought about Saturday, or talked about it, she wouldn't be able to hide her fear.

When the children were all in bed, she came back into the kitchen to unload the dishwasher and wipe down the cabinets. Ryan followed her in and grabbed the broom, beginning to sweep.

"Didn't you have fun today?"

"Yes, of course. Oh, I'm going to buy a carrot cake from Katie's bakery for Saturday. It's fabulous. I know you'll love it."

"Yeah, I've tasted it. But you're as good a cook. Why not just make something?"

"I have a lot to do for Saturday, and I don't want to run late or not get things done." She paused and then added, "If it bothers you, I'll pay for it with my money."

"Damn it! You know that's not what I mean. You've got to stop spending your own money. Or I'm going to have to start paying you a salary."

She was already ill at ease from the events of the day. When tears started seeping out from under her closed eyes, she was horrified. As was Ryan when he saw them.

"Susie, don't cry! What did I say? I take it back, whatever it was. I don't want you to cry."

"You said you'd pay me a salary, like I'm not part of the family," she said as she sobbed.

"Hell and damnation, I didn't mean—Susie, you're the center of this family. You make everything possible. The kids adore you, and I do, too. Don't ever think that." He had his arms around her, pulling her into his hard chest, kissing every part of her face that she hadn't covered. "Come on, Susie, look at me. You know I didn't mean that."

She looked up to nod to him and he kissed her lips. The embrace went deeper and deeper, and Suzanne felt lost in his arms in a wonderful spiral of pleasure.

Then he stopped and set her aside. "Everything's going to be all right, sweetheart. But you look a little tired. Why don't you go get ready for bed?"

"That—that's a good idea," she said shakily. If they talked much longer, she might break her vow and tell him her fears. Besides, the sooner she slept, the sooner he'd hold her again.

He gave her a quick kiss on her lips, nothing like their earlier embrace, and she smiled before she went to their bedroom.

RYAN KNEW he was in trouble now. After holding Susie like that and kissing her more intimately than ever, he knew he couldn't slide into bed and hold her all night without doing what he'd promised he wouldn't do until she was ready.

So what was he going to do now? He guessed he'd get a sleeping bag and head for the barn for the night. He'd be up before anyone else in the morning. If one of the cowboys saw him there, he'd think he was checking on something before breakfast. And the children didn't get up as early. He might even get back in the house before Suzanne got up. He'd change shirts so she wouldn't realize he'd been out all night.

He found a sleeping bag in the hall closet, left there for when they stayed out overnight when they were doing roundup. He put it on the kitchen table. Then he filled a thermos with the leftover coffee and grabbed some of the cookies Suzanne always had on hand and put them in a plastic bag.

Figuring Suzanne would be asleep by now, he quietly opened the door to the bedroom. He heard her even breathing. Creeping over to his closet, he stripped off his shirt and grabbed another. He stood there snapping it up.

"Are you going somewhere?" a soft voice asked.

He whirled around. "I—I thought you were asleep."

"No."

"I'm going to the barn to check on something."

"And you changed your shirt because the horses require formality?" She had pushed up on one elbow, her long hair falling on her shoulders. She looked as sexy as hell.

"Uh, I spilled something on it at dinner. I didn't

want to get it any dirtier,'' he assured her, as if his words made sense.

Suzanne got to her feet and grabbed her robe off the foot of the bed. She pulled it on and walked out of the bedroom to the kitchen. She stopped cold at the sight of the sleeping bag.

"And the sleeping bag? The horses want company?"

He couldn't come up with anything that made sense.

They stood there in silence. Finally he decided to tell the truth. "I decided to spend the night in the barn because...because I can't trust myself in the face of so much temptation."

"What temptation?" she asked, her eyes innocent.

He groaned. "Didn't you even notice what just happened in here, when you started to cry? Another minute and I would've taken you on the kitchen table. I promised I'd wait until you're ready. I don't want to break my word. I'll be fine in the barn with the bedroll. It won't be the first time I've spent the night out there."

"But—but you said we had to share a bedroom so our marriage would appear real."

"No one will know."

"You don't know that. And rumors could do us in."

He grabbed the bedroll and his thermos and cookies and headed for the door.

"Wait, I don't want you to go."

"Honey, I'm telling you I have to go, or I'll make love to you. I'm a healthy male."

He backed away from her toward the door, as if she couldn't stop him if he faced her.

"But I don't want you to go."

"Are you listening? Susie, I—"

"Yes."

"Well, then—"

"I want you to make love to me."

Ryan took a deep breath, not moving. Then he said, "What did you say?"

"I want you to make love to me."

"You're sure?"

"Yes, Ryan, I want you to—to love me…if you want to."

He gave a shout of laughter. Then he swooped down on her, dropping the bedroll, thermos and cookies on the table. "Oh, honey, I'm sure. I'm so very sure. Come on. Let's go to bed."

SUZANNE COULDN'T BELIEVE she'd had the nerve to tell him what she wanted. But if he was going to risk his life on Saturday, she wanted to be loved by him now. After her father's abandonment of her and her mother, she'd been a needy girl, looking for a man who would stay. But apparently her neediness drove her to pick men who wanted nothing to do with permanence. Ryan, on the other hand, had every intention of being around for the next fifty years. Not that he was dedicated to her, but he was dedicated to his land. So she could trust him to stay.

And she loved him.

When he looked at her, a twinkle in his blue eyes and a grin on his handsome face, she would do anything for him. When he cradled Mandy against him, teased Beth out of her bad moods, or taught Josh things he needed to know, her legs went weak and she loved him more than ever. When he slid into bed, thinking she was asleep each night and pulled her against him to hold her safely through the night, she trusted him. Completely.

They reached the bed and he stopped her from getting in. "I think you're wearing too many clothes. I know I am. Let's get naked before we get in."

She gulped and nodded her head. She took off her robe, then took hold of the highest button of her pajama top and slowly worked it free. Then she looked at him. He'd grabbed his shirt and ripped all the snaps open.

"Need some help?"

Her cheeks reddened. "I—I didn't know we were in a hurry."

"Oh, yeah, honey. I'm in a hurry. I've waited every night since our wedding to make love to you." He pulled her to him. Then he reached for her next button. He slowly unbuttoned it, his gaze never leaving hers, even though he'd said he was in a hurry.

Then his gaze dropped to her breasts and he ripped the buttons apart all at once. The satiny material slid down her arms, and she stood in front of him naked from the waist up.

"Oh, Susie!" he said with passion, and his lips

found hers. That kiss made their earlier embrace in the kitchen seem innocent. Her breasts rubbed across his chest and tremors shook her. He was hot and hard and she wanted to curl around him forever.

He stopped kissing, his chest heaving, to unzip his jeans and slide them down strong legs. Before he could get them off, he had to get his boots off, too. While he was hurriedly doing that, Suzanne slid down her pajama bottoms and her panties. She stood patiently waiting for him, stark-naked.

He could hardly breath, she looked so pure and beautiful. And desire made his hands all thumbs. Finally, he, too, was rid of the irritating clothes. He pulled her to him, running his hands up and down her body.

Then he lifted her into the bed and joined her there. Finally, he was going to love his wife the way she should be loved.

Their intimacy increased rapidly. While Suzanne appeared a little inexperienced, she didn't hesitate to encourage him. He loved it! He loved every inch of her for as long as he could stand it. Then he plunged into her, ready to take her to the greatest high he'd ever experienced, he was sure.

But there was something she'd forgotten to tell him.

Chapter Thirteen

"Susie! Why didn't you—I can't—"

"Don't stop, please," she said urgently, clinging to him.

He didn't. It would've been virtually impossible even if he'd tried.

A few minutes later, he lay exhausted on the bed beside her. He gathered his strength and sat up. "Damn it, Suzanne, why didn't you tell me you were a virgin?"

"I don't remember you asking. You just assumed I'd 'been around,' right?" She was embarrassed at his reaction, and none too comfortable sitting around naked. She pulled on her pajamas, her back to him.

"I would've been more gentle if I'd known."

"Or not touched me at all."

"I'm sure I—I wanted you. You knew that."

"So I cooperated. What's the problem?"

"Well, one I hadn't thought of is birth control. Knowing you're a virgin, I wouldn't have assumed you're on the Pill." He gave her a hard stare that didn't fill her with happiness.

"No, I'm not! I don't recall you asking me about that either."

"Well, you didn't ask about a condom. Most women will even provide them."

"Sorry. I don't have your *experience!*"

"Damn it, you may already be pregnant. And if there's one thing we don't need, it's another kid!"

That statement pierced Suzanne's heart. She'd opened her heart to Beth, as she had to Josh and Mandy. Now he was telling her he didn't want *her* baby? She grabbed her robe and left the room.

A moment later, he followed her. "What are you doing?" he demanded, staring at her stretched out on the lumpy mattress in the first room she'd occupied.

"Go away. I don't want to talk to you. I don't want to listen to you and I surely don't want to touch you." She turned over so her back was to the door and waited to hear him leave.

He stood there for several minutes, breathing heavily. Finally he left, closing the door behind him. Suzanne let out the breath she'd been holding. Unfortunately, that also seemed to release some tears. She sobbed quietly for a while. Then she wiped her face and tried to think of the future. She loved him. But she wasn't sure she could stay married to him. She'd thought making love with Ryan would be heavenly. But she'd had in mind the soft cuddling, the sweet nothings, the…togetherness. Ryan didn't bother with those things. He satisfied himself and then chewed her out.

Why hadn't she told him? Well, duh. "Oh, by the

way, this will be the first time, okay?'' That would've stopped him cold. Men didn't like to be the first one. They felt guilty afterward.

Well, let him feel guilty. And if she was pregnant? She would be delighted to have a baby. It wouldn't make her love the other three less. But clearly Ryan didn't feel that way. So, when she found out if she was pregnant, she guessed she'd have to take the children and leave. Beth, too, if she wanted to go.

What she'd thought would be a glorious occasion gave her heartache and tears and a lack of sleep. No one told her it could be like that.

WHEN THE LIGHT crept into the bedroom the next morning, Ryan slowly awakened. The immediate sense of loss when he discovered he was alone brought back the events of last night. He hadn't handled the situation like he should've. But he'd been embarrassed and upset. He'd hurt her and that made him feel even worse. Worst of all, he'd told her he didn't want her baby. He'd known when he'd said it that it was the wrong thing to say. But he was in the middle of a custody fight. He couldn't think of another baby right now. Later. Later would be great. But he hadn't planned on a baby right now. But he still knew he'd played the fool, and he would have to do a lot to make up for that statement.

When he realized it was 6:15 a.m. and Suzanne wasn't in the kitchen, he thought about waking her up. But he couldn't face her. So he got dressed and put on a pot of coffee. He found a plate of blueberry muffins in the refrigerator. Taking two out, he heated them in the microwave and had them with his coffee. Still no movement in the house.

He got a piece of paper and a pen and tried to write a note. After scratching out several things, he wrote, "I'm sorry. I made some mistakes last night. I'll make them up to you." Then he signed his name and left the kitchen, his coffee cup rinsed and put in the dishwasher.

Instead of joining his cowboys, he drove into Cactus, hoping to join Cal and Mac at The Lemon Drop Shop. He needed male advice.

They were there with Gabe, Katie's husband. Ryan knew him, but not well. He joined them anyway.

"Mind if I sit down?" he asked, pulling out a chair.

"Of course not," Cal said, smiling at him. Then he looked at the others. "Uh-oh, we've got troubled waters in sight."

"Yeah. Marriage isn't a snap of the fingers," Ryan said glumly.

"Sure it is," Mac said with a grin. "But it takes a guy a while to figure out that he isn't the one who gets to do the snapping."

Gabe was grinning and Ryan wanted to hit him.

As if reading his mind, Gabe pushed away from the table a little bit. "I'm only laughing because I suffered some when I first got married. Katie had to train me a lot."

So Ryan forgave him. "Mine doesn't want to train me. She wants me to go away." He ducked his head. He hadn't known that was going to come out. And Suzanne hadn't told him to go away, except last night when she wanted him to get out of her room. Surely she didn't really mean forever. That would ruin everything.

"What's the judge going to say if she leaves me?" he asked desperately, grabbing Mac's attention at once.

"Leave you? She's thinking of leaving you?"

"I don't know."

"You wouldn't have a chance if your second marriage is falling apart," Mac said grimly, his lips pressed together.

"Why would she leave you?" Cal asked, leaning forward.

Ryan lowered his voice. "We made love last night...for the first time. She wanted to wait until she was settled in."

"You did marry in a hurry, one of the grandmother specials," Gabe said. He'd had one, too, so it wasn't a criticism.

"I know. And I agreed to wait. But I made her cry earlier and when I comforted her and apologized, I got carried away. So I couldn't get into bed with her and *not* make love to her. So I was going to the barn to sleep."

"Good man," Cal said quietly.

"But she told me not to go. That she wanted me to make love to her."

He stopped there and the other three men leaned closer.

"Isn't that good?" Mac asked.

"So good I forgot everything. I took her to bed and it was great, but then…you know…I discovered she was a virgin."

"Uh-oh. Here comes the problem." Cal leaned back in his chair. "You got angry, didn't you?"

"Well, hell, yes! She should've told me. I would've been more gentle."

Mac scratched his neck and stared across the square. Gabe hid his mouth and Ryan suspected he was grinning. Cal had tipped his cowboy hat down over his face.

"You boys need anything else? Well, hello Ryan. You want something to eat or drink?"

"A cup of coffee would be good, Katie. I'll come in and get it myself."

"Nonsense. We're not too busy this morning. I'll be right back." Katie hurried inside.

"Your wife is nice," Ryan said to Gabe.

"So's yours. The whole town is talking about how lucky you got this time, not marrying another Tiffany," Gabe said. "If she leaves you, they're going to begin to suspect the problem is you." Ryan gave him an angry glare.

"Come on, now," Mac said softly. "If any of us got what we deserved, all our wives would leave us. So let's calm down and figure out how to straighten things out."

Katie came back with a dish with several sausage rolls on it, an empty cup and a full pot of coffee. "Here, boys, I'll let you pour your own cups, okay? We've got a sudden rush."

"Thanks, sweetheart," Gabe said.

Then he looked at Ryan. "Can't you just go home and apologize, take her flowers or something?"

"I—I could if that was all I'd done."

"Good lord, there's more?" Cal asked, raising his eyebrows.

Ryan hurried through what he knew was the worst part. "We didn't use birth control, and I said the last thing we needed was another baby."

The other three men were silent, their faces reflecting their realization of how serious a mistake he'd made. None of them spoke.

"I know," Ryan finally said. "It was a terrible thing to say. She's loved Beth from the first moment, and Josh and Mandy, too. If I get to keep Beth, it will be because of Suzanne. But I didn't mean it. I meant, right now. Right now with this challenge for custody of Beth. I don't have time to concentrate on anything but Beth." He was practically pleading when he finished, hoping if he could convince these men, maybe he'd have a chance of convincing Suzanne.

Mac shook his head. "That's weak, Ryan. By the way, did you straighten out the problem with Mother's Day Out?"

"Yeah. I apologized. I was wrong."

"Um… You've got another problem…" Cal said slowly. "I told Jessica I wouldn't tell, but you're in enough trouble as it is."

"What are you talking about?" Ryan asked.

"Your wife is almost hysterical over the thought of you riding any of the bulls tomorrow."

"That's silly!" Ryan protested. "You know I do

it all the time. I'm careful. And I've never been hurt.''

''Okay. Now think of it from Suzanne's point of view. She's not used to rodeos. I understand her father abandoned her and her mother when she was around nine or ten. Then her mother died. She moved in with her aunt and uncle and grew up like a sister to Mary Lee. Then Mary Lee and Rodger die. She leaves her city job and comes to a new place to take care of her cousin's orphaned children. Then she gets rushed into marriage. Things go well, and she starts having feelings for the man. Then he wants to risk his life for a macho thing. And she's gonna be left with three children who will be devastated, and perhaps she will be, too.''

They all sat there in the morning sunshine, thinking about Cal's words. Ryan wanted to throw up. He'd never thought of it from Suzanne's point of view. If he followed his usual pattern, he would ride three or four bulls, maybe a bucking bronc or two and accept the accolades of his friends and strut into the house to brag to his wife. And she'd be trembling, fearing disaster, because that's what she'd come to expect. Talk about an insensitive clod!

''Who told you this?'' Mac asked.

''Jess, of course. And I'm breaking my promise to her not to tell you. But you had to know what was going on in Suzanne's head. She turned white as a bedsheet yesterday and began shaking, her voice rising. Samantha got her some carrot cake and made her eat it. She was afraid she'd go into shock.''

"And they didn't think I should know that?" Ryan demanded, ready to challenge someone right then.

"She begged them, with tears in her eyes. She didn't want you to be embarrassed by her silliness. Said she needed to adjust." Cal stopped there and sat silent for a couple of minutes. Then he added, "Ryan, you've got a great wife. Don't screw it up."

Ryan sighed and dropped his head.

Mac said, "Not that you're not a catch yourself. We know you're a good man. It's just hard for us guys to understand what goes through the heads of women. But that remark about not wanting her baby was a major goof."

"So what do I do?"

Again there was silence. Gabe picked up the coffeepot and poured Ryan some coffee. Then he refilled the others' mugs. "Katie might think we didn't like her coffee if she came back and found the pot still full."

"So, what *are* you going to do?" asked Cal.

"Fall on my knees and explain and apologize. And not ride any bulls tomorrow because I hurt my knee working. How's that?" Ryan said.

"It's a start. You didn't really hurt your knee, did you?"

"Naw. But it will take care of things for tomorrow."

"I think that will work," Mac said. "I haven't ridden much lately, so I won't be trying them tomorrow, either. Let the young ones take the spills."

All the men agreed, and Ryan felt bad. He hoped

they weren't denying themselves the thrills because of him. He thought about that for a minute and realized it didn't thrill him much anymore. He rodeoed because he was expected to, not because he enjoyed it. That was a big discovery. Maybe he'd enjoy himself more if he didn't ride. He could visit with friends, watch those bulls more closely so he'd know what to do about them, and help keep an eye on the kids. He could show Josh what was going on and help him understand so he wouldn't want to go rodeoing some day. He had to think about his children's future.

WHEN RYAN CAME IN for lunch, he approached slowly. Opening the back door, he made a little racket as he came in and the children came to surround him. He greeted each of them, as he always did.

"Let Dad go wash up, kids, so we can have lunch," Suzanne called from the kitchen. Same words as usual. But Ryan thought he detected a lack of warmth.

He washed and came back in to find everyone at the table waiting for him. Suzanne was in her usual place, between Josh and Mandy, with Beth between Ryan and Mandy. She didn't look up.

Ryan bent his head and asked a brief prayer. He tried to catch her eyes. But she'd turned her attention to Mandy, filling her plate for her. She encouraged Beth to eat her vegetables. She supervised Josh in his choices. She ignored Ryan.

He noticed she picked at her food, eating almost nothing. She served dessert, but she didn't eat any.

"Not hungry?" he asked casually.

"No." No anger. Just indifference.

"I can't wait to see you ride the bulls tomorrow," Josh enthused.

"Son, I may have to disappoint you," Ryan said hurriedly as Suzanne started out of the room. She paused. "I hurt my knee while I was riding this morning. I think I won't try to ride tomorrow. I have to be able to take care of my cattle, you know. I can't get laid up because I was playing."

"Oh," Josh said, disappointment in his voice. "I understand, Dad."

"Good boy. Maybe another time." He took a bite of lunch. "But there will be others, a lot younger, showing off. It will be fun."

Suzanne came back to the kitchen sink and began rinsing the dishes making lunch had required. Then she gathered their dinner plates and dessert bowls.

"Isn't it quiet time?" Ryan finally asked. Suzanne had said nothing about it.

"Not yet," she said now. "I'll put them down in a minute."

"I want to pitch in. I'll put them down," he insisted, realizing she was avoiding any time alone with him.

When he came back into the kitchen, she was gone.

Where had she gone? He found her in the porch swing on the back porch, sitting quietly, with a glass of iced tea in her hands.

"You didn't eat much. Are you feeling all right?" he asked

"I'm fine," she snapped, no appreciation for his concern.

"Suzanne, I want to apologize for last night. I was embarrassed that I'd hurt you because I was so—eager to make love to you. It was all my fault. I apologize." She said nothing.

"I promise the next time we make love, it will be more…pleasurable for you. But I won't touch you again until you want me to. Just—just let me know."

Nothing.

"I also apologize for the remark about not wanting a baby. What I meant was right now. I want to concentrate on keeping Beth right now. Later, if you want a baby—or more than one baby—I'll be happy to oblige you."

"Thank you. I won't require that much sacrifice from you."

Well, his rehearsed apology hadn't warmed her up much. She still sounded bitterly angry.

"Sweetheart, I hated hurting you. And I hated that stupid remark the minute I heard myself. I promise that's not what I meant."

"The main thing," she said in precise words, "is that you're right. We need to concentrate on the custody challenge. I wouldn't be holding up my end of the bargain if I don't help you keep Beth."

He moved quickly and sat in the porch swing with her before she could object. "Thanks, Suzanne. I knew I could count on you. About the other, you know, making love, we'll take it at whatever speed you feel like.''

''I think the speed I choose is reverse,'' she snapped and got out of the swing to disappear into the house.

Damn. He'd apologized nicely and also refused to ride the bulls tomorrow. What more could he do?

Then he remembered. He had to keep his word to Josh. He went back in the house. She glared at him. ''What do you want?''

''I promised Josh I'd take him with me this afternoon. I need to keep my word.''

''He's already resting.''

''I bet he's thinking I forgot him,'' he said as he started down the hall. About that time, Josh's door flew open and the little boy came running down the hall. ''I forgot. Ryan is supposed to take me riding,'' he called.

''Sssh,'' Suzanne warned him. ''You'll wake the girls.''

''I'm here, pal. I remembered after you went to your room. I came back for you.''

''You really will? You weren't teasing?''

Ryan smiled at the boy. ''No, I wasn't teasing. A cowboy keeps his word.''

''Oh, boy, I'm ready!'' Josh exclaimed.

''No, you're not. Go put on a long-sleeved shirt so you won't get sunburned. And your boots, of course. Do you have a hat?''

''No!'' the boy exclaimed, concern in his voice.

''Maybe I have an old one you can wear. Then you'll be ready. We have to protect ourselves.''

Josh tore down the hall to do what he was told and Ryan started for the hall closet where a lot of things were stored.

Suzanne stopped him. "Ryan, thank you for not disappointing Josh."

"I wish I hadn't disappointed you, honey. If there's anything I can do to make it up to you, please tell me."

She looked away.

After a moment, he dug in the closet and came up with a hat he'd had when he was younger. It wouldn't fit Josh exactly, but he could use it today. Tomorrow morning, he needed to take the kid to town and get him his own hat. And the girls, too.

What about Suzanne? She didn't even have boots yet. Maybe they'd all go shopping tomorrow morning. He suggested the idea to Suzanne.

"I need to remain at home and finish getting ready for our guests. My friends are coming early."

"Oh, of course. Well, I'll take the kids out of your hair and we'll pick up fast food for all of us for lunch. Okay?"

"Whatever you would like," she said stiltedly.

"Suzanne—"

"I'm ready, Dad. Wow, is that a hat for me?"

"Yeah, son. It will be a little big, but it will do for today. I'll buy a you a new one tomorrow."

"Oh, boy! I'll be a real cowboy, then."

"Yeah. Tell Mom bye."

Josh ran to hug Suzanne and she squeezed him tight. "Be careful, Josh."

"We will, Mom. Bye!" He was out the door without waiting for Ryan.

"I'll take good care of him," Ryan assured Suzanne.

"You'd better," she warned, concern in her eyes as she stared after the boy. That's why she didn't notice Ryan's approach. He kissed her lips and was out the door almost as fast as Josh.

Chapter Fourteen

Suzanne had actually done most of the work for tomorrow, so she had some free time on her hands, which meant she could worry more about Josh. He was too small to ride alone, in her opinion, but if Ryan took it easy with Josh in front of him, everything should go well.

But she couldn't help worrying that something might not go well. Concentrating on Josh kept her from thinking about her own situation with Ryan. She didn't want to think about it. There was too much going on. She planned on sleeping in the little room by herself until the hearing forced her to do otherwise.

When the phone rang, she thought maybe it was Ryan calling on his cell phone. Instead, it was Mac Gibbons.

"Suzanne? I tried to reach Ryan on his cell phone but there was no answer. Is he there?"

She spotted his cell phone on the charger just as Mac said that. Ryan had forgotten to take it with him. "No, he forgot to take it, Mac. May I take a message?"

"Sure. I just got word from Joe Walton, the judge who will hold the hearing about Beth's guardianship. The social worker will be out Monday. Then the hearing will be Wednesday."

Suzanne gasped. "Will you be ready that quickly?"

"I think so. And don't worry. All you and Ryan have to do is impress the social worker. Everything going all right?"

"Uh, yes, of course," she lied. "Everything's fine."

"Good. I'll see you tomorrow."

"Yes. I'm looking forward to it." Another lie. Right now, she wished they could have the weekend to themselves.

She hung up the phone, knowing what she had to do. Move back into Ryan's bedroom. And make sure there was absolutely no sign of her having occupied the little room.

By the time she'd finished those chores, the girls were awake and asking for a snack. She had even found a way to establish in the girls' minds where she slept.

"Oh, Beth, I need my dust mop. I think I left it in Mommy and Daddy's room. Would you get it for me please?"

"Okay," Beth agreed cheerfully and ran directly to her father's bedroom. She brought back the dust mop. "You get to share Daddy's bedroom?" she asked.

"Yes. That's what husbands and wives do."

"Oh. What's our snack?"

"How about cookies and milk?"

"I thought we didn't have no more cookies," Beth said.

"Any more, sweetie. But we do. I just baked some, and you two can help me bake the rest of them."

"Where's Josh?" Mandy asked, frowning.

"He went out with Ryan. They'll be back in a while and you can give both of them cookies that you made. Won't that be great?"

Mandy agreed that it would, though she still looked a little unsettled. But once she got to make cookies out of the dough Suzanne had mixed, she forgot about her brother.

About an hour later, Ryan and Josh came in. "You're early," Suzanne said, smiling at both of them. "Did everything go all right?"

She could see the surprise on Ryan's face at her congenial greeting. She wanted to tell him why, but she couldn't. Not until they were alone. Or maybe she could. She'd just have to couch her words in a way that the children wouldn't understand.

While everyone had some cookies, she said, "Mac called."

"Oh. I forgot my cell phone."

"Yes. We'll have a visitor Monday and then the next part on Wednesday." She kept any emotion from her face. "Here Josh, Mandy made this one especially for you," she pointed out.

"Did you ride a horsie?" Mandy asked her brother.

"Yeah. Me and Dad rounded up the cows," Josh said importantly. "It was great!"

"I think I used to go with Daddy," Beth said, a puzzled look on her face.

"You did, Beth, when you were smaller. I had to work and you were too young to leave behind." He smiled at his daughter and then turned to Suzanne.

"Is everything okay?"

"He said so. Said he'd see us tomorrow."

"Okay. Is there anything I have to do for our Monday visitor?"

"Who's coming?" Beth asked.

"A lady. They want to be sure I'm a good Mommy."

"You're the best Mommy!" Beth exclaimed.

"Thank you, sweetheart. I try."

"Beth's right," Ryan said, a smile on his face. "You are definitely the best Mommy."

"Thank you." She turned the television on for *Sesame Street* and tidied up the kitchen from the snack. The children all turned their attention to the television. Ryan joined her at the sink.

"Did Mac say anything else?"

"Not really. He said for us to do our part on Monday."

"I know you're not happy with me, but I hope you'll pretend to share my bedroom."

"I've already moved back in and cleaned the extra bedroom thoroughly," she assured him, not looking at him.

He patted her arm. "Thank you, Suzanne. I'll keep my promise."

"Thank you." The only thing that bothered her was whether she could keep her promise to herself. Making love to Ryan had been an emotional disaster. But the physical side of it had had its moments.

But she should keep her distance since she'd decided she couldn't stay if she was pregnant. Of course, if he used a condom…she shook her head. She couldn't do that.

"What?" Ryan asked, evidently having watched her.

"Nothing. I was just thinking." She moved to wipe off the table.

"Are you sure you can't come with us in the morning?" Ryan asked, following her.

"No, I don't think so. All my friends said they'd be here early to help. I wouldn't want them to come and find me gone."

"I see."

As the evening progressed, the children grew more excited about shopping in the morning with Daddy. They discussed the hats over and over again. Mandy proclaimed she wanted a red one. Even Suzanne couldn't hold back a chuckle at that thought. "Sweetie, I don't think you should get a red one," Suzanne said calmly. "A bull hates the color red. He might chase you if he saw a red hat."

"Would he catch me?" Mandy asked. "I run fast," she added, staring at Suzanne.

"I'm afraid bulls do too and they're lots bigger than you."

''Oh. Okay, I get a white hat. Do bulls like white hats?''

''White is a good color for bulls,'' Ryan said with relief.

Suzanne was glad when it was time for the children to go to sleep. She wouldn't have to listen to a discussion of hats again. But it meant she and Ryan would be alone. She didn't want to discuss anything with Ryan.

She came back in the kitchen and pulled down her lists for the next day. She had planned every step. She'd bought sodas and planned to make tea. She looked up as Ryan came back into the kitchen.

''Can you pick up four bags of ice when you start home tomorrow with the children?''

''Sure. Will it be enough?''

''I hope so. Alex and Tuck are bringing four also. I've rounded up four coolers. I'm going to put sodas in those and fill them with ice. And I'll use the other four bags for the iced tea.''

''Shall I pick up the cake from Katie's bakery, too? Or have you already gotten it?''

''That would be nice. I was planning to go to the bakery tomorrow morning.''

''Anything else I can do for you?''

''No, thank you.''

He poured himself some more tea and sat down at the table. He seemed happy to sit and stare at her, but Suzanne couldn't stand that. ''How did Josh do today?''

''He did great. He was nervous at first. But he

began to feel the rhythm of the horse and got his balance.''

''You held on to him, didn't you?'' she asked.

''Yeah, but he's a natural, Suzanne. Next week I'm going to start him riding a pony.''

''Maybe not next week. There will be a lot of pressure on all of us next week.''

''True. On Wednesday, can you find someone to keep the kids?''

''Yes. Will Beth have to be at the hearing?''

''I don't know. I'll ask Mac tomorrow.''

''I might let Josh come, if he wants, too. But Mandy will definitely need a sitter.'' She hadn't thought about it, but she thought Josh was entitled to know what was going on.

''I'll leave those choices up to you,'' he said.

She nodded but said nothing. She didn't know how long she could use her lists as an excuse to avoid him. She already knew them by memory.

She remembered that a show she liked to watch was coming on TV. She moved over in front of the television and turned it on. That should keep Ryan from talking to her.

''You like this show?''

''Yes, it's one of my favorites. Do you like it?''

''I've never seen it.''

It started right then, so she shushed him. By the time it was over, he was watching as intently as she was. ''Hey, that's a good show.''

''Yes. Next week should be good. There's another show I like on Wednesday nights we could try— Oh, that's the day of the hearing.''

"Yeah."

"I'm sure you'll win, Ryan."

"*We'll* win," he emphasized.

"Yes, of course."

"You still haven't forgiven me, have you?" he asked suddenly.

"I don't think we need to discuss that subject right now. I'm doing what I can to help you keep Beth. I promised that."

"Okay. Time for bed."

His sudden declaration startled her. "I—I think I'll have some cookies and milk now. I didn't eat any earlier."

"Good. I'd like some, too."

Rats. She hadn't planned on him staying up with her. "Maybe…I've changed my mind. I don't need the calories."

"Don't be ridiculous. You're not a bit over-weight. And you haven't eaten enough the last couple of days to keep a bird alive."

"Obviously," she said dryly, "that's not true, or I'd be dead." She got up and poured herself some milk. She offered some to Ryan, but he said no. Then she put some cookies on two plates. There was an awkward silence as they ate the cookies. Suzanne kept her gaze straight ahead and chewed stoically. Ryan tried a little conversation, but when she didn't respond, he too fell silent.

Fifteen minutes later, she knew if she got up to go to bed, he would follow her. She didn't want him in the bedroom while she prepared for bed. She got a break when the phone rang.

"Yeah, Mac. Suzanne told me you called."

When Suzanne heard that, she figured he'd be on the phone a little while. She scurried to the bedroom and quickly dressed in a nightgown. Then she brushed her teeth and washed her face. When she came back into the bedroom, Ryan still wasn't there.

She got into bed, with only the bathroom light left on for Ryan and settled down to sleep. Much to her surprise, the tension had been so great all day, that it took no time to fall asleep.

When Ryan came in ten minutes later, she was breathing evenly, her eyes closed. He got ready for bed and got in beside her. He was glad she was asleep. He needed to hold her tonight, to draw strength from her. She couldn't protest what she didn't know. He pulled her against him and sought much-needed rest.

THE SUN ROSE on a beautiful day Saturday morning. Everyone slept a little late. Ryan got up first and put on a pot of coffee. He wanted to be out of bed before Suzanne woke up. He didn't want any discussion of their sleeping positions.

When they'd had breakfast and the kids were dressed, Ryan took all three of them in his truck to town. Suzanne walked them out to his dual cab truck and made sure they all got buckled in.

"Be sure you buckle up for the trip home, too. Okay?"

"Yes, Mommy," Mandy answered for all of them. "Bye-bye."

Suzanne stepped back and waved goodbye, a sudden lump in her throat.

Ryan, standing beside her, must have sensed her distress. He leaned over and kissed her cheek. "I'll bring them back safely, Mom."

Then he got in the truck and drove them away.

It was amazing how much her life revolved around her three children. She'd only had them for a month or two. But they meant everything to her.

She piddled the rest of the morning away. Then she spent extra time on her appearance. She dressed in a long patio dress in blue, her favorite color. It's loose, casual lines were comfortable and made her feel glamorous. She tied her reddish-brown hair back with a matching blue scarf. Then she added a little makeup. She added sandals and gold earrings, and a big spray of her favorite perfume. Just as she set the bottle down, she heard Ryan's truck.

She hurried out on the porch. He was helping the children down from his truck, each of them sporting a cowboy hat. The children ran to Suzanne to tell her about their shopping. Ryan unloaded the ice, making two trips to get the ice into the kitchen. Then he went back for the carrot cake.

When he finally came back out on the porch, he said, "You sure look good, Suzanne. Doesn't Mommy look pretty, kids?"

Beth frowned. "I need a dress. I want to look pretty."

She headed for her bedroom.

Suzanne stopped her. "The only reason I'm wearing a dress is I don't have a cowboy hat, Beth. You need to wear jeans if you're going to show off your new hat.''

"Oh," Beth stopped, still frowning.

"I hungry!" Mandy announced, not concerned about her jeans.

"Yikes, I forgot our hamburgers," Ryan said with a laugh. "Thanks, Mandy. I'll get them."

"And you three go wash up," Suzanne ordered. Then she followed Ryan to the truck to help with the lunch.

By the time they'd finished eating, Mac and Samantha had arrived with both their children. Cassie was Beth's age and they enjoyed playing together. Their son was two years old, the same as Mandy. Suzanne sent them to Beth and Mandy's room, asking Josh to supervise them.

"That sounds good," Samantha said with a sigh. "They've been so excited all morning. I think Mac is more patient with them than I am."

Mac grinned. "I keep a file when she says things like that. Then, when she's unhappy with me, I remind her of what she said."

"Maybe I'll start one," Ryan said, looking at Suzanne.

She was fixing iced tea for everyone and ignored him.

"I wanted to tell you, Suzanne, in case you're worried about Monday. I know the social worker well. We've worked on cases together before. She's very nice."

"Oh? That's good to know, but I think we're fine. What's her name?"

''Marilyn Carroll. She actually lives in Lubbock. The court doesn't want someone who lives close by and already knows you. They're afraid it might prejudice the report.''

''That makes sense,'' Suzanne agreed with a sigh.

''Well, the house sure looks good,'' Mac said. ''While Ryan was on his own, it was barely habitable.''

''Come on now,'' Ryan protested, ''it wasn't that bad. Just—dusty. And, um, no decent food in the house. I sure chose the right woman to fix all that, though, didn't I?''

''That you did,'' Mac agreed, smiling at Suzanne.

''Well, if you decide to have other children, I'd advise a housekeeper. A woman can only do so much,'' Samantha said.

''Don't worry,'' Suzanne said. ''We've decided not to have more children.'' Her words were clipped and it was obvious there was a story behind them, but Samantha didn't say anything.

Fortunately, they heard new arrivals and discovered Cal and Jessica with their children.

As they waited for them to unload and reach the house, Suzanne asked Samantha. ''How is Jessica feeling?''

Before Samantha could answer, Ryan asked, ''Is something wrong with Jessica?''

''No,'' Samantha said calmly. ''But she's three months pregnant. They're hoping for a girl.''

''I forgot she was pregnant. I guess I assumed they'd stop at two.''

"That's a good number," Mac said, avoiding Samantha's gaze, "but I'll admit I'd like more."

"You would?" Ryan asked, surprised.

"Yeah, but that has to be Samantha's decision since it affects her more than me. But I believe when you've got the money to support a family, you should have all the kids you can. Children that would be well fed, cared for and disciplined. Kids that will grow up to be the leaders of the future. Or you could adopt the abandoned ones. We've actually talked about that."

Jessica and Cal knocked on the back door. The children were directed to the children's rooms and Suzanne fixed more iced tea for their guests. "How about some oatmeal raisin cookies to go with the tea?" she asked.

"Terrific!" Cal exclaimed, as if he hadn't eaten in months.

"I swear, some day, all his calories are going to catch up with him," Jessica complained. "Right now he eats like a horse and it never shows on him."

Everyone laughed. Cal's appetite was legendary. Suzanne fixed two plates of cookies, one for each child's room. Then she filled a plate with cookies for the adults.

"Want me to deliver these plates?" Ryan asked, getting up to help.

"That would be nice, thank you." Suzanne ignored all the stares from their friends.

"You might try not being so polite on Monday," Mac suggested casually.

"Of course," Suzanne said, taking his advice seriously. "Maybe I should've said, 'Thanks, honey.' Is that better?"

"Yep, it is. But I'm sure you'll do fine," he added with a smile.

"Way to make her feel relaxed," Samantha said. "Just ignore him, Suzanne."

"I'll try. Oh, there's Melanie and Spence and Alex and Tuck."

All the men jumped up as Ryan came back into the room. "Melanie and Spence and Tuck and Alex are here," Cal said. "Spence and Tuck are anxious to see those bulls of yours. Ready to show them?"

"Sure," Ryan agreed. Then he paused. "Do you mind, Susie?"

"No, of course not. Go ahead."

He stepped closer and kissed her. Then he headed for the door.

"Is he practicing for Monday?" Jessica asked.

"Yes, of course," Suzanne said with a sigh. "Otherwise, we probably wouldn't be speaking."

Chapter Fifteen

As much as Suzanne had dreaded the day of the rodeo, everything went spectacularly well. She enjoyed visiting with the other women. They took turns keeping an eye on the children. When Josh and his friends wanted to go watch the rodeo, Suzanne went with them. She watched the men riding the bucking broncos. She even saw some of them riding the bulls, though she found it much more dangerous.

When Josh and his friends wanted to go back to the house, Jessica took them back. Suzanne didn't really want to see any more riding, so she wandered to the back of the arena where some of the animals were in temporary corrals. She leaned against a truck parked nearby.

Suddenly she heard voices.

"Hey, Ryan, why aren't you riding today? You're not afraid the challengers are better than you?"

"I guess that's it," Ryan said with a laugh. "Actually I banged my knee yesterday, and I didn't want to hurt it worse today."

"I haven't noticed you limping," the unknown man said.

Come to think of it, neither had Suzanne.

"Okay, you caught me. My wife's had a lot of changes in her life because of tragedy. She was uneasy about me riding, and I decided it would be better not to this time. I may ride again another time, but I've got to take care of my wife."

Suzanne's jaw dropped. Had someone told him? Even if they had, Ryan had found a way to make her feel better without making her feel guilty.

"Well, as pretty as your wife is, I guess taking care of her isn't hard."

"Nope. And the rewards are terrific," Ryan said. Suzanne could hear his grin.

She wanted to rush around the truck and hug his neck. She thought again about the reasons she loved him. As Mac said, she needed to keep a file so she wouldn't forget what a considerate man he was.

"I bet!" the man agreed with Ryan with a laugh. "You're lucky you moved fast. A lot of the guys noticed her at once. But they politely gave her time to settle in. That was their mistake."

"Yeah. It was lucky that circumstances—and the grandmas—made fast work of things."

Suzanne slipped back to the house. She didn't want to thank Ryan in front of his friends. But she would thank him.

Everything was calm in the house. Jessica was in charge. She didn't want to stay outside long.

"Besides, when you've seen one crumpled cowboy, you've seen enough,'' she added as Suzanne sat down.

''Have we had any injuries?'' Suzanne asked hurriedly.

''One cowboy broke his arm. But that happened when he lost his balance and tumbled off the rail. He's known for being a klutz, poor thing. The others tease him all the time.''

''Oh, my. He must be miserable,'' one of the other ladies said. ''My husband was sure he wanted to ride a bull, but after he saw Ryan's bulls in action, he changed his mind, thank goodness. If I didn't enjoy these days so much myself, I'd protest about coming.''

''Oh!'' Jessica said. ''I promised Samantha I'd remind everyone of the schedule for parenting classes this summer. Florence and Sam are doing them again, but on Tuesday evenings.''

''They do them together?'' Suzanne asked.

''Yes. It seemed to Florence that if you have to study rules to drive a car, you should have preparatory classes for parenting. They started the classes three years ago.''

''That's a wonderful idea. Maybe I should sign up,'' she said, frowning.

Everyone laughed. ''You're doing a fine job,'' Melanie said quietly as the laughter stopped. ''I think you're okay.''

About that time, Mandy came running into the kitchen, making a straight shot to Suzanne's lap. ''Mommy! That boy pulled my hair!'' She buried her face in Suzanne's lap. Suzanne lifted the child to straddle her legs. "Did it hurt, sweetie? Let me rub it."

Jessica stood and headed for the bedroom.

"Jess! It's okay. Don't—"

"No. It's the only way they learn. I'll be right back."

Suzanne consoled Mandy and told her to lie against her and close her eyes.

Before Mandy could doze off, however, Jess came back in with her youngest boy. She came to a stop in front of Suzanne.

"Okay, tell her."

"I'm sorry I pulled your hair," the boy snuffled, his head down.

"Good. Now come sit in time out."

Suzanne felt so sorry for him. But she didn't argue with Jess. Discipline was necessary.

Mandy fell asleep against her and Jess finally let her son go back to play with the others. "He's lucky I'm the one to punish him. Cal goes berserk if the boys hurt smaller children, especially girls. If this one is a girl, I'm going to have to work hard to keep him from spoiling her."

Not a minute later, Cal and Ryan came into the kitchen. "Everyone's hungry. How long 'til dinner?" Ryan asked Suzanne.

"If you'll take Mandy and put her on our bed to finish her nap, we can get things ready in about half an hour. Will that do?"

"Perfect!" he said as he bent to kiss her lips and then take Mandy from her. He cuddled the little girl against him and left the room.

"How have the boys behaved?" Cal asked, looking at Jessica. "They haven't caused you any trouble?"

"No, honey, they've been fine."

"I told them not to wear you out."

All the women laughed as Jessica soothed her husband. Ryan came back in and the two men went to the arena to tell everyone dinner was in half an hour.

Suzanne began heating dishes. Fortunately, she had two ovens. The iced tea had been mixed and put in a huge dispenser that they'd get the men to put on the end of one table outside.

Paper plates and napkins were ready.

"We're lucky there's no wind today." Melanie said, smiling. "One year, Suzanne, a huge wind blew up. All the paper plates and cups started blowing away unless they were full. We all had to hang on to everything."

"That sounds miserable. Why don't we put the desserts here on this table? Then we won't have to worry about them drawing flies while we eat. And when people are ready for desserts, they'll be waiting for them."

"Good idea," several women said and began taking their cakes, cookies and pies and setting them out. They began carrying out the meats and veggies. Some were refrigerated, like the deviled eggs and coleslaw. The cheese and macaroni in a huge container was heated, as were the mashed potatoes and gravy. There was so much food, including fried chicken and barbecue beef, Suzanne wasn't sure they could even make a dent in it.

But she was wrong. The cowboys had worked up a huge appetite. Two hours later, there were barely any leftovers.

Ryan set down a piece of carrot cake in front of Suzanne. "I grabbed the last piece for you, sweetheart."

"Oh, thank you, Ryan, but I'm so full—"

"You deserve it. Everything was great."

"But I wanted you to have some."

"I'll take a bite of yours." He opened his mouth and waited. She scooped up a bite and put it in his mouth. Then he bent down and kissed her. "It's no sweeter than you," he added.

She thought he was overdoing the playacting, but she said nothing.

The children were kicking around a rubber ball like a soccer ball, and the adults, full and satisfied, watched them expend energy the adults could only remember.

After the sun set, everyone began cleaning the area and loading the picnic tables in the backs of trucks, wrapping up remainders to take home and locating their dishes.

When they were finally left alone on their back porch, still waving goodbye, Suzanne sighed. "What a wonderful day."

Ryan's arm came around her. "Yeah, it was. Thanks to your hard work."

"I didn't do much. Kids, did you have fun?"

They agreed they had, but it was obvious they

were tired. "Okay," Suzanne said, "Girls, let's go take your bubble bath. And Ryan, will you supervise Josh's shower? I expect a clean neck, young man, okay?"

Josh grinned and sheepishly said, "Okay, Mom."

Once they were out of the bath, the girls dressed in their pj's and quickly fell asleep. Ryan hardly worked in a good-night kiss for each of them beforehand. Josh, too, fell asleep quickly.

"Nothing like a full day to put them to sleep," Ryan said with satisfaction.

"Yes, it was a full day. And they love their hats, Ryan."

"I should have thought of them before. And you, young lady, don't even have boots. Though I prefer your sandals, we've got to take care of that deficit. By the way, can you ride a horse?"

"I have done it, but not much. But I probably won't need to."

"You never know on a ranch. That's like having a swimming pool and not learning to swim."

"Well, it's not quite that bad," she protested.

"We'll start riding lessons for everyone," he said firmly.

"Even Mandy? She's too young."

"No, she's not. You don't want her to feel left out, do you?"

"No, of course not."

"Well, then, that's what we'll do."

"Let's wait until after Wednesday."

"Are you worried?" he asked softly.

"No, of course not, but—but we'll all be distracted until then."

"I suppose you're right. I think I'll take a shower and get ready for bed. I'm as tired as the kids," he added. With a smile, he kissed her lips and headed to the bedroom. Darn, she'd have to wait until he finished before she took her shower. Then she remembered the children's bath. She gathered her gown and robe and clean underwear and headed for a well-deserved bubble bath.

She took her time in the bubble bath, enjoying it as much as the girls did. When she finally got out, some of her tension had disappeared. She'd intended to thank Ryan for not riding today, but she wouldn't mind putting it off until tomorrow. Her resistance was a little low tonight.

She tiptoed into the bedroom, thinking Ryan would be asleep. But he was sitting up in bed, reading. His chest was bare and she drew a deep breath.

"I thought you'd be asleep," she said.

"I thought I would, too, but I guess I've gotten used to having you beside me."

He gave her a slow smile, one that stirred her senses. The man was impossible to resist. She tried to shift her mind to something practical, but she couldn't do it. Finally, she said what she'd planned to say. "I want to thank you for—for not riding today. I don't know who told you about my fears, but I didn't want you to leave yourself open to teasing."

Instead of answering her, he said, "Aren't you going to get into bed?"

She turned out the light and shrugged off her robe. Okay, if he didn't want to talk about his behavior, she was fine with that.

She got into bed, keeping strictly to her side. Just as she settled down, his long arm hauled her up against him.

"Ryan!"

"I just wanted to tell you that all you had to do was ask me not to ride. To explain it to me."

"I thought I made it clear that I didn't like the idea."

"Yeah, but I thought it was because you're a city girl, that was all. I hadn't considered your concern in the light of all the tragedies you've lived through. Hell, I owe you so much already, you should've known I'd do what you wanted."

Ah. He owed her. She'd hoped for so much more. The fact was, she was in love with Ryan Walker. And he owed her.

"Well, I appreciate it," she simply said and tried to put some distance between them.

"Susie, I know you're here because of Beth, but I want to love you. I'll be gentle this time, I promise, now that I know how inexperienced you are. Will you trust me?"

She bit her bottom lip. "Do you have a condom?"

"Yeah, if you want me to wear one."

She was already trembling, eager to feel his touch, but afraid she was making a mistake. She nodded.

He sat up and opened a drawer in the bedside table on his side and pulled out a foil-wrapped package. He was already enlarged, eager to touch her. He put on the condom and then reached for her.

He was right. He was gentle and made sure she was ready for him this time. The pleasure was immense for her. Afterwards, he drew her into his embrace, her head on his shoulder, and closed his eyes. Within seconds, it seemed, he was asleep.

Suzanne debated if making love with Ryan had been a mistake. In the end, she told herself it had hurt no one except maybe herself. It made her want him to love her more. But at least she'd had a good experience this time. If she was going to have to leave, she would at least have that to remember. Slowly her eyes settled and her debating lapsed. She fell asleep in his arms.

WHEN RYAN came to the breakfast table the next morning, he first came around the table and swept Suzanne into his arms for a drugging kiss. She was glad they were going to church this morning. If they'd had any extra time, he'd have had no trouble leading her back to bed.

"Do the kids have their clothes ready for church?" he asked as he sat down at the table.

"Yes, both girls have their dresses from the shower to wear, and Josh has his dress pants and a nice shirt."

"You probably need to take the girls shopping for more clothes when you have time. I know Beth doesn't have much of a wardrobe, and I think Mandy's been growing lately."

"I know. Maybe we'll do a little shopping tomorrow. I don't— Oops! I guess that won't work since the social services lady is coming tomorrow.''

"It's a good sign that you almost forgot. Means you're not too nervous," he said, smiling at her.

"I think our home life is okay."

Before she could continue, Ryan grinned at her. "I'm liking it!"

She knew what he meant, and her cheeks turned red. She didn't want to discuss what they had done in bed last night. She was still not convinced it had been a good idea. But she hadn't been able to resist him. "I meant our meals and the activities I do with the kids."

"No one could complain about that either," he assured her, still grinning.

"Go wake up the kids," she ordered, determined to change the subject.

He did as she asked. In a few minutes he came in, carrying Mandy, who still seemed asleep. Beth came wandering in behind him, rubbing her eyes.

"Where's Josh?"

"He's coming. Or at least he'd better be." Ryan put Mandy in the chair that had the booster seat. Then he walked to the door and yelled, "Josh!"

That roar produced a result, as Josh came in in his pajamas. He crawled up on his chair and put his head on the table.

Suzanne patted his head. "You still tired from yesterday? We let all of you sleep later this morning."

"More," Josh mumbled.

"No. We're all going to church together this

morning, remember?'' She set their food on the table and joined them there. ''Everyone eat a good breakfast and you'll feel better.''

''When you get old like me and Mom,'' Ryan said, ''you'll handle these things better. Look at us. We're wide-awake.''

Suzanne was tempted to say something, but she decided the topic of bed was best avoided. ''After church, maybe we can talk Dad into taking us to The Last Roundup for lunch. How about it, Dad?''

''I think that's a fine idea,'' he said cheerfully, making no resistance at all. ''Mom should have Sunday off, shouldn't she?''

''Thank you,'' she said politely, ignoring that grin that kept reminding her of last night.

She was proud of her little family when they collected in the kitchen to leave. Both girls looked so cute in their new dresses. Suzanne had put their hair in ponytails and then used the curling iron so the ends curled. Josh, with his new haircut, looked nice, too. And Ryan, well, he was as handsome as ever. If he weren't married, he'd have all the women chasing after him.

They all got into Ryan's truck with the dual cab. Josh and Beth sat in the narrow back seat with Mandy belted in her car seat between them.

''You know, many more kids, and we'll have to buy a bigger car. An SUV or something like that.''

She was astounded by Ryan's remark. He knew there weren't going to be any more babies. He'd made his opinion about more babies completely clear.

She said nothing and looked out the window beside her.

Josh, however, made the request he'd already made once. "Can we have a boy this time, so I'll have someone on my side?"

"We can try," Ryan said, grinning.

Suzanne glared at him.

"But not right away," Ryan hurriedly added.

They rode silently the rest of the way into town. When they'd placed each kid in his or her own Sunday-school class, Ryan led Suzanne into the couples' class.

Their friends were already there and hurried over to tell them how much they'd enjoyed the day at their house. Suzanne thanked them for the compliments, but her mind was on Ryan and the remarks he had made in the truck.

"Is everything all right?" Jessica asked, aware that they didn't really have Suzanne's complete attention.

"Oh, yes. In fact, Ryan promised to take us to the Last Roundup for lunch."

Everyone around Suzanne agreed that they, too, would eat lunch there. Jessica stood. "I'll go get a table for all of us before they start to fill up."

"Good idea, hon," Cal called, apparently overhearing her remark. "It pays to know the owner," he added with a big grin.

Everyone laughed. What a perfect marriage Cal and Jessica seemed to have, Suzanne thought. And they were having another baby. In fact, all their friends seemed to be happily married. She wondered if they all thought the same about her and Ryan.

There was a lot going on under the surface that she and Ryan didn't reveal. She hoped her friends were truly happy as she and Ryan wanted to be.

After church, they enjoyed a long lunch with their friends. When they headed for home, the motion of the truck put Mandy and Beth to sleep. Even Josh was fighting to stay awake.

They put the two girls in their beds and told Josh it was quiet time. He went without fussing. When Suzanne checked a few minutes later, she discovered him fast asleep.

She decided a nap would be a good idea for her, too. She didn't feel quite up to par. She lacked her usual energy. She took off her panty hose and shoes, hung up her dress and slipped into a robe. Then she lay down on the bed.

Before she could get to sleep, however, she was joined by Ryan. He had something besides sleeping on his mind. She found the pleasure increased each time he loved her. Was he being extra careful? Or was she growing more attracted to him? Perhaps it was a combination of the two.

When he pulled the cover over both of them, she had no trouble falling asleep.

Chapter Sixteen

Suzanne had stayed up late Sunday evening, planning her day to impress the social services worker. She had every detail ready for examination, and everything designed to prove what good parents she and Ryan were.

The social services worker had called and asked permission to come at 7:00 a.m. Naturally, Suzanne had agreed. Not to do so would make it look as if she had something to hide.

She planned to get up at her usual time, 6:00 a.m., and prepare a good breakfast and bring the children to the table as soon as the lady arrived.

When she awoke Monday morning, her plans went out the window. She'd overslept.

"Ryan! Wake up! It's almost seven-thirty."

"The boys will tease me a little, Susie. But that's okay."

In her frustration, Suzanne slugged Ryan in the arm. "Miss Carroll is supposed to be here already. Get dressed!"

She slid into her robe and ran for the back door.

She assumed the lady sitting in the porch swing was Miss Carroll.

"I'm so sorry, Miss Carroll. We overslept. Please come in."

"Don't be upset, Mrs. Walker. That happens." Marilyn Carroll had a lovely smile, and Suzanne drew a deep breath.

"I'll get the coffee on at once. Have a seat at the table," she said.

Ryan came into the kitchen, tucking in his shirt-tail.

"Ryan! You should finish dressing in the bedroom!" Suzanne snapped.

"I *am* dressed!" he roared back at her, irritation on his face.

Suzanne turned her back on him and began cooking the bacon and making toast. "Miss Carroll, would you care for some eggs this morning?"

"Oh, no, I've already had breakfast, Mrs. Walker."

"Please, make it Suzanne. We're not formal here."

"Surely, if you'll call me Marilyn."

Ryan stuck out his hand to the lady. "I'm Ryan, which I guess you figured out. We don't often over-sleep, and it's got Suzanne rattled a little."

Suzanne ground her teeth, refraining from chastising her husband for his remarks.

She slid a couple of eggs, sunny-side up, onto a plate and put it in front of him. "Eat while it's hot," she muttered. Then she took out three coffee mugs and poured the coffee. "Do you take cream or sugar, Marilyn?"

"No, just black. And it smells wonderful."

Suzanne smiled, relaxing just a little. "Thank you. I'll let Ryan entertain you while I wake up the kids."

She thought the look on Ryan's face, a combination of irritation and surprise, was payment for his mentioning her being rattled. She ducked into her room first and pulled on a pair of jeans and one of Ryan's cowboy shirts, leaving the long shirttail out. After running a comb through her hair, she went into Josh's room. "Honey, wake up and get dressed. We've got a guest for breakfast so you have to get dressed first. I'm laying out what you should wear."

"Okay," Josh muttered and turned over, snuggling down again.

"Josh, I want you up and getting dressed, *now!*"

The boy jumped and sat up. "What?"

"We have a guest for breakfast. Get dressed and comb your hair before you come to the table."

"Oh, yeah, I 'member," he acknowledged. She'd explained about Miss Carroll coming the night before.

She repeated the message to the little girls. She helped Mandy get into her play clothes and supervised Beth. Then she sent them to the bathroom. "I'll be waiting for you in the kitchen."

As soon as she came into the kitchen, Ryan jumped up and excused himself. He put his arm around Suzanne's waist and kissed her goodbye. Then he was gone.

"I hope he used good manners," she said, watching Miss—Marilyn, carefully.

"Of course he did. But he was anxious to get to the barn and make sure his manager got the men assigned to the right jobs. Typical rancher."

"Yes," she agreed with a sigh. She scrambled some eggs for the children and herself. "Sure you don't want any eggs?"

"No, but if there's enough bacon and toast, I'll munch on that."

"Of course. Help yourself."

The children came to the table and Suzanne introduced them each to Marilyn. They all looked adorable, in her opinion. She hoped Marilyn thought so too.

After breakfast, she told them to go make their beds and straighten up their rooms while she cleaned the kitchen.

"May I observe the kids while they do that?" Marilyn asked.

"Of course," Suzanne agreed, crossing her fingers.

She breathed a sigh as she began cleaning the kitchen.

She had finished the kitchen and grabbed the opportunity to mix up some brownies quickly. She'd just put the pan in the oven when she heard a painful shriek from the children's bedrooms. She slammed the oven shut on the brownies and raced out of the kitchen.

Marilyn and Josh came out of his bedroom. They all entered the girls' room at the same time. Mandy was lying on the floor, holding onto her right arm. Beth was staring at her with a look of fear on her face.

Suzanne wasn't concerned with who had done what at that moment. She wanted to determine how badly hurt Mandy was. It only took a minute to discover that Mandy's right arm was broken.

She picked up the baby and carried her into the kitchen. "Josh," she called as she sat down with Mandy in her lap. "Call the bunkhouse and tell Al I need him. And call the barn and tell Daddy to come back."

The little boy did as directed. Beth stood at the door, afraid to come into the kitchen.

Suzanne had stopped Mandy's shrieks and comforted the child. Now she called to Beth. "Come here, sweetie."

Beth reluctantly came forward.

"What happened?"

"I didn't do nothing!" Beth shouted.

"She pushed me!" Mandy said and then whimpered as she moved her arm again.

"Beth, I want you to tell me the truth, please," Suzanne said calmly.

"She was messing up my dollies that I keep on my bed, and I—I pushed her away to make her stop. And she fell."

By the time she finished speaking, her little chin was quivering. She burst into tears. "I didn't mean to hurt her!"

Suzanne put one arm around Beth. "I know you didn't, honey, but we need to deal with things like that differently. Next time, could you come tell me what is wrong, instead of pushing Mandy? Then I could explain to Mandy that she can't mess with your things. Wouldn't that be better?''

Beth rubbed her wet cheeks. "Yes, but I didn't mean to hurt her."

"I know."

About that time, Al knocked on the back screen door.

"Come on in, Al. Marilyn, this is Al. Al, Miss Marilyn Carroll. I need to take Mandy to the doctor, Al. Will you be able to watch Josh and Beth while we're gone?"

"Sure," Al agreed.

"Thanks. Josh, did you talk to Daddy?"

"No, he'd already left the barn, but one of the guys was going to find him."

"Try his cell phone, Josh. That would be faster." She told him the number to dial. "I should have that on the wall by the phone," she muttered.

"Daddy?" Josh exclaimed. "Mandy's hurt and Momma needs you to come back."

"She broke her arm," he explained after a moment. "Okay."

Then he hung up the phone. "Daddy's coming."

"Thanks, Josh. You did that very well. Oh, Al," she began, then paused. "Oh, no. I left the brownies in the oven too long. Al, could you—?"

Al got up and pulled the pan out of the oven. The brownie's edges were black.

"I'm sorry, kids. I made those up for snack

time,'' Suzanne wailed, thinking she couldn't have looked worse in Marilyn's eyes.

''I'll make some more, if you have another mix,'' Al assured her.

''Thank you Al. That would be wonderful.''

Then she noticed Beth sulking in a chair across the table. ''Beth, could you get me a blanket to wrap around Mandy? She's getting cold. I think she's in shock.''

Beth scrambled down and ran down the hall. She hurried back with one of the blankets from Mandy's bed.

''Thank you, Beth. That was very helpful of you.''

''Here comes Daddy,'' Josh said as he peered out the screen door. ''He's still riding his horse. Is he going to ride his horse to the doctor?''

''I don't think so,'' Suzanne said. She twisted so she could see Ryan. He was riding with another man. When they reached the porch, he slid off the horse and gave the reins to the other man. The cowboy led the horse back to the barn.

''How is she?'' Ryan asked.

''I think she's fallen asleep. Beth brought me a blanket to wrap her in and Josh called you and Al. He's going to watch the kids while we take Mandy into the doctor's.'' Then she turned to Marilyn. ''I'm sorry about leaving. If you want to leave and come back tomorrow, that will be fine.''

''No. If you don't mind, I'll go on with my observation.''

''Of course,'' Suzanne said, trying to hold on to

her composure. "Children, *Sesame Street* comes on in five minutes. After you watch it, you have half an hour of work. Then Al will fix you a snack. Okay?"

"Yeah," Josh said seriously. "You'll get Mandy well?"

Ryan put his hand on the boy's shoulder. "We'll do our best, Josh. But it may take a while. We'll need to discuss how it happened when we get back."

Beth ran from the room, crying. Suzanne said, "It was an accident, but Beth blames herself. She pushed Mandy away when she was bothering her things. Go talk to Beth quickly. I'll call the doctor while you do that. Then we need to go."

When they were finally in the truck, the children and Marilyn came out to see them off. Suzanne pulled the seat belts around them. Then she sighed as Ryan pulled onto the county road.

"Not exactly how I intended this day to go."

"Accidents happen. However, I still need to talk to Beth about using her strength on smaller children." Ryan's lips were pressed tightly together.

"Beth didn't intend to hurt Mandy."

"I know that, but she shouldn't be pushing her around."

Suzanne said nothing. She was growing more and more concerned about Mandy's apparent sleep. Had she hit her head? Was she in an unconscious state?

"You okay?" he asked.

"Me? I'm fine, but I'm worried about Mandy going to sleep. And I'm worried about what Marilyn thinks of us.''

''It'll be all right. It's not your fault.''

She said nothing. There was nothing to say until she knew whether Mandy would be all right.

The nurse stood behind the desk as they entered the office. ''Come right in. Dr. Hausen is waiting for you,'' she said with a smile.

Suzanne came to an abrupt halt. ''Dr. Hausen? But I thought—I mean, I wanted to see Dr. Gibbons,'' she said, naming Samantha.

''She's not on duty today,'' the nurse said, looking at Ryan uncertainly.

''It's okay, honey. Jeff is a great doctor. He married Diane, Katie's sister. You'll like him.'' He put his arm around her waist and urged her forward.

Ryan was right. She did like Jeff Hausen. He was very gentle and calming with Mandy. And he reassured Suzanne, too.

''You've got a clean break. It will only take about six weeks to heal. We'll put her arm in an arm cast.'' He said after taking X rays. ''Of course, keep her down for a day or two and give her baby aspirin if she complains of pain. A lot of milk to drink won't hurt,'' he added with a grin.

''Thank you so much, Doctor,'' Suzanne said. She smiled at him.

Ryan stepped forward to put his arm around her again. ''Anything I can do?'' he asked.

''You might cut down on your work hours for a few days, give Suzanne a hand. You'll probably have some jealousy problems, as Suzanne will have to spend a lot of time with Mandy. Does she still take a nap?''

"Yes, for a couple of hours," Suzanne said.

"Lucky you. Any questions?"

"No, thank you."

When they got back in the truck, she put Mandy in the center seat belt and then slid in beside her. "You can lean against me, sweetheart."

"Where's Daddy?" Mandy asked in a slurred voice. About then Ryan opened his door after helping them in. "I'm here, Mandy. What do you need?"

"I want to lean against you," the little girl said.

Suzanne closed her eyes, fighting the jealousy that filled her. The doctor had mentioned the other children being jealous. She hadn't realized she, too, would feel that way.

"It's because she doesn't see me as much," Ryan said softly, touching Suzanne's shoulder.

Embarrassed that he'd known what she was feeling, she smiled. "Of course."

She borrowed his cell phone and called home. Al answered the phone and immediately asked about Mandy. Suzanne assured him Mandy was fine and asked him to tell the children. He told her he'd fixed sandwiches for lunch and the children were eating now.

"Thank you, Al, you really pitched in. I appreciate it."

Suzanne turned to Ryan and said, "The kids are eating now. When we get there, we'll be able to send them to their rooms for nap time."

"Good, I'm going to talk to Beth before she goes to sleep."

Suzanne started to protest, but then, Beth was his daughter, not hers. That thought changed her mind. "If you feel you must, okay. But she already knows what she did was wrong, even though it was an accident. I think it would be better to wait until after Wednesday."

He frowned. "You think so?"

"What if you lose custody? I don't want to think about it, but she would think you didn't want her anymore because she made a mistake."

"No! How could she—"

"She's three years old. She needs to be reassured that you still love her, Ryan."

"Well, of course I do!"

"She's three," she repeated.

After a moment of silence, he said, "Okay, I guess you're right."

His agreement made Suzanne feel much better. They *were* a family, after all.

THAT NIGHT, after they had tucked the children into bed, Suzanne led the way back into the kitchen and poured three more cups of coffee.

"Come sit down, Marilyn."

"Thanks," the lady said with a sigh. "It's been a long day."

Ryan frowned and Suzanne knew she looked panic-stricken.

Marilyn looked up and saw their responses. "Oh, no, don't take that the wrong way. I meant because of Mandy's accident. We all worried about her until we got the phone call. I'd like to reassure you that I didn't see anything negative on my visit. You both showed loving attention to the children even in the worst of circumstances. You showed concern for Beth and Josh as much as Mandy. You also showed a good reliance on each other. In fact, my report will be one of the best I've made this year. I don't know your ex-wife, Ryan, but you have a wonderful wife now.''

Suzanne blushed and Ryan reached out for her hand lying on the table.

''I know I do.''

''I understand you aren't much of a cook or housekeeper though. So it's a good thing you got married,'' Marilyn said to Ryan with a chuckle. ''Otherwise you might have lost your little girl.''

''But you don't think I will, now?'' Ryan asked.

''No. Not at all. In addition to Suzanne on your side, you've got a good lawyer. Mac is another point in your favor.''

Ryan grinned. ''Yeah. He's a fighter for the good guys.''

''Yes, he is. So, I'll see you both in court on Wednesday. What are you going to do with Mandy and Josh?''

''I'm going to see if Florence can keep Mandy for the day, but we're thinking of letting Josh come with us for Beth's sake,'' Suzanne explained.

''That's a good idea. I'll see you all there and we'll try to take care of the matter.''

"Thank you," Suzanne and Ryan said together, shaking Marilyn's hand as she rose to leave.

"She's right, you know," Ryan said, looking into Suzanne's brown eyes. "I was saved by our wedding."

Suzanne said, "I might have already lost the ranch by now if I hadn't married you. When the children try to thank me for keeping their inheritance safe, I'll have to refer them to you."

"Well, the fact is, we're a family now. In every sense of the word." He scooped her up in his arms and she grabbed at his shoulders to stabilize herself.

"Ryan! What are you doing?"

"I'm taking my wife to bed!"

THEY DIDN'T OVERSLEEP Wednesday morning. Both Suzanne and Ryan were very quiet. After breakfast, Suzanne took Beth to her room and dressed her in a pretty dress and fixed her hair in a curly ponytail. "You look so pretty, Beth. Daddy will like how pretty you look."

"Do I have to wait for him to tell me?" she asked anxiously.

"I'm afraid so. But I'm sure he will. Now I'm going to dress Mandy in her play clothes and then we'll be ready to go."

"How come Mandy gets to go play and I don't?"

"Daddy explained it last night. The judge needs to ask you some questions."

Suzanne dressed Mandy, who still fussed about her arm cast. Then she took the two girls to the kitchen where Josh, dressed in slacks and a dress shirt, and Ryan, in a dark suit, sat waiting. Ryan's knuckles were white and Suzanne put her arm around his shoulders.

She whispered, "Tell her she looks pretty."

"My goodness, look at these two beautiful girls, Josh," Ryan said at once.

Josh, frowning, looked around. "Where?"

Suzanne had to hide her laughter. "Your sisters, Josh."

"Oh, yeah. You look pretty too, Mommy."

"Thank you, darling," she said, bending to kiss his cheek.

"Hey, you're showing me up, Josh. I think Mommy looks beautiful, too," Ryan said.

Suzanne bent to kiss his cheek, too, but he took her lips instead.

But she didn't protest. She knew how nervous he was.

After dropping Mandy off at Florence's house, they drove to the courthouse in Lubbock. Several of their friends had made the effort to be there, which they appreciated. Mac was at the table on the right and waved for Ryan and Beth to come to him. Ryan again kissed Suzanne before he took Beth's hand and went to join Mac. Suzanne led Josh to the first row behind the rail, so that they were as close to Ryan and Beth as they could be.

It was almost ten o'clock, the time for the hearing to begin when Tiffany and a stern-looking man swept into the courtroom. She was wearing a blue fox stole over a bright pink suit that was tight as could be. She had a tiny hat with pink veiling over her heavily made-up face. And, of course, her fingers were covered with flashy rings.

The man with her wore an expensive business suit. The frown hadn't gone away. He sat down beside his wife and looked around. When his eyes lit on Beth, he smiled. Ryan's hands tightened on his little girl. Suzanne leaned forward and patted his shoulder.

They all rose when the judge entered. Once they were seated again, the judge asked Marilyn Carroll to come forward and make her report.

It hadn't occurred to Suzanne that Marilyn would spend Tuesday with Tiffany, evaluating her home. She listened to what Marilyn had to say.

"To sum it up, your honor, the Walkers are a family, with life centered around their children. Mrs. Ritter is a socialite with a full schedule centered around her wardrobe and her beauty salon. I saw no indication that she desired a change."

Suzanne relaxed for the first time.

"I protest!" Tiffany said, leaping to her feet. "Your Honor, I can't have children. I had to find something to fill my lonely life. All Carl does is work."

"Mrs. Ritter, your lawyer is supposed to talk for you. Do not speak out of turn again."

Tiffany gracefully sat down, sending a look of suffering to the judge.

Then the judge called Tiffany to the stand. Her lawyer asked the questions necessary for her to expand on her loneliness and her need for a child. Then it was Mac's turn.

"Mrs. Ritter. Will you please tell the court why you are unable to bear children?"

"You can't ask me that!" Tiffany snapped.

"Young lady, I believe this is my courtroom. I make those decisions." The judge pointed out.

"Well, I don't want to relive those painful moments."

"I'm afraid you'll have to."

Chapter Seventeen

"I—I had a horrible pregnancy. It was very painful, so I asked the doctor to tie my tubes."

"I see," Mac said, showing no surprise. "We'll come back to that subject in a little while. When you left your husband, how old was Beth?"

"Six months old."

"Did you receive visitation privileges?"

"Yes, of course."

"When was the last time you saw her?"

"A couple of weeks ago," she said with a smile.

"That was after you had filed for the custody hearing?" Mac asked casually. She smiled and nodded her head.

"And before that? How old was she the last time you saw her before that visit?"

Tiffany looked at her lawyer, who was frowning. Finally, she said, "It had been a while. I have a lot of responsibility as Carl's wife."

"Just give me an estimate of time," Mac suggested, smiling gently at her.

"Well, a while."

"Would it be two and a half years?"

Tiffany wiped her face clear of any emotion. "Yes."

"So you haven't been back to see your child since the day you left her when she was six months old?"

"That's right. I've been busy."

Still easygoing, Mac said, "What did you get her for Christmas last year?"

"I don't remember such details. We gave presents to the orphanage near us. I bought a lot of presents last year."

"You didn't in fact send her a present, did you, Mrs. Ritter?"

"I'm sure her father bought her something."

"And her last birthday? Did you buy her something then?"

"No."

"When is her birthday?"

"Uh, October."

"The date?" Mac prodded.

He had moved so he stood between her and her lawyer. Tiffany tried to look for help, but she couldn't see through Mac.

"Your Honor," her lawyer said, standing. "I object to this line of questioning. Mrs. Ritter's lack of ability to recall details doesn't mean she doesn't love her child."

"Let's move along, Mr. Gibbons."

"Yes, sir. Mrs. Ritter, do you remember your visit to the ranch two weeks ago?"

"Of course I do!"

"Did you tell Mr. and Mrs. Walker that you

would take either Beth or the other little girl, that it didn't matter as long as you got a child?''

"No! Of course not!''

"I object!'' the lawyer said. "He's putting words in her mouth.''

"Overruled,'' the judge said, leaning forward to watch Tiffany carefully.

"Mrs. Ritter, may I remind you that you are under oath?'' Mac stared at her. "I have two witnesses to your statement. Three actually, because Josh heard you also.''

"Who is Josh?'' Tiffany asked.

"The little boy sitting with Suzanne Walker.''

"You're going to believe a child instead of me?'' she demanded belligerently.

"Yes,'' Mac said calmly.

"I may have said something about not knowing which one was Beth because it had been a long time since I saw her, but that's normal.''

"No more questions now, Your Honor, but I reserve the right to recall this witness.''

The judge nodded. Then he looked at Tiffany's lawyer. "Any questions?''

The man got up and ran through a few questions about Tiffany's love for her child, hoping to present a different image.

"Next witness?'' the judge asked Mac.

"Yes, I'd like to call Beth Walker.''

Ryan got up to take his child to the witness stand. Tiffany's lawyer protested, saying he would influence the child if he was holding her.

Suzanne could tell Mac wasn't surprised. "Your

Honor, may I offer my wife as a substitute for Ryan Walker? She is Beth's doctor.''

The judge cleared it with the other lawyer and Samantha stepped forward. She greeted Beth and picked her up. She sat down on the witness stand and put Beth on her lap, her arms securely around her.

Mac approached them. ''Beth, how old are you?''

Beth held up three fingers.

''Three? My, you're a big girl.''

She nodded.

''Do you have any brothers or sisters?''

''Josh and Mandy,'' she promptly said, pointing to Josh.

''Do you enjoy playing with them?''

She nodded again.

''Do you have a mommy and daddy?''

She nodded and pointed to Ryan.

''Do you love them?''

''Lots and lots,'' the little girl said with enthusiasm.

''Do you do special things with your mommy?''

She nodded. Then she held out her hands. ''She paints my fingernails. See?''

''Yes, I do. Very nice. Does she take you shopping for pretty dresses?''

''Yes. I picked this dress all by myself. Mommy says I have good taste.'' There was light laughter that ran through the courtroom and the judge hit his gavel. ''Quiet.''

Beth, bug-eyed, stared at him.

"He didn't mean you, Beth. You're supposed to talk," Mac explained.

Beth looked at the judge nervously, but Mac smiled.

"What else do you do with your mommy?"

"She teaches us to cook. And to color and—how to spell. I can spell cat," Beth added proudly.

"Really? How do you spell cat?"

She did so confidently. But she added sadly. "I can't spell dog yet. I forget."

"You'll learn soon," Mac said.

"That's what Mommy says," Beth said, smiling brightly.

"And just to be sure we all know her, point to your mommy," Mac said. Beth did so, and Mac added, "Let the record show that Beth is pointing to Suzanne Walker."

"Beth, I just have one more question. Who is that lady, the one in the pink suit?"

Beth looked over at Tiffany. "I don't know. She's a lady."

"Thank you, sweetheart. Why don't you go back to your daddy for a few minutes."

Beth got down with Samantha's help and ran back to Ryan.

"Your Honor, I'd like to keep my wife on the stand as a witness."

"Swear her in," the judge ordered.

After she was sworn in, Mac addressed her as Dr. Gibbons. "Dr. Gibbons, when a woman has her tubes tied, is it irreversible?"

"No. With the new laser surgery, I believe there

has been quite a bit of success reversing the surgery that Mrs. Ritter had.''

''I protest!'' But it wasn't the lawyer who stood. It was Tiffany. ''I'm not going to get pregnant again. I'd lose my figure and have to go through those nights when she doesn't sleep all night. And changing diapers and spitting up. It was disgusting!''

The judged rapped again and insisted, ''For the last time, Mrs. Ritter, sit down and remain silent.''

''Thank you, Dr. Gibbons,'' Mac said with a smile.

''Next witness?''

''Mrs. Suzanne Walker.''

Suzanne jumped. She hadn't expected to be called. She squeezed Josh's hand. Melanie was sitting on the other side of Josh and she nodded at Suzanne, promising to look out for Josh.

Suzanne was sworn in and she took the chair on the witness stand.

Mac asked, ''Suzanne, when did you marry Ryan Walker?'' Suzanne gave the date.

''Was Ryan a good father before you married him?''

''Oh, yes. He and Beth are very close. But then, he's a good father to all three children. He's gentle and generous with his time to all three.''

''You're not prejudiced, are you?'' Mac asked with a grin.

''Probably,'' she said with a smile. ''I became a parent overnight when my cousin and her husband were killed in a car wreck. But I love these three children. We've become a family.''

"Do you think Beth is a well-adjusted child?''

"Yes. And she's accepted me easily. She and Mandy share a room and we've had very few problems.''

"Thank you.''

The other lawyer strode to the witness stand. "You're hiding something, aren't you?''

"I beg your pardon?'' Suzanne asked in surprise.

"Beth and Mandy had a fight, and Beth broke Mandy's arm.''

The man looked at her triumphantly.

"Mandy has a broken arm, correct. It happened accidentally when Beth pushed her away from her dollies. But there was no intent to harm Mandy. The two have become very good friends.''

"Does she always break the arms of her friends?'' the lawyer sneered.

Suzanne drew a deep breath. "That's a ridiculous question. Accidents happen to children, and that's exactly what it was, an accident. If you knew anything about children, you'd understand that.''

The lawyer opened his mouth for a rebuttal, but the judge rapped again. "Move on, counselor.''

"Nothing else,'' the lawyer said.

"Mr. Gibbons, do you have any more witnesses?''

"No, Your Honor.'' Mac said and sat down.

The other lawyer also declined to call any more witnesses.

"Closing arguments in fifteen minutes.'' The

judged rapped his gavel and stood, leaving the courtroom.

Suzanne returned to her seat. Ryan assured her she'd done well. Beth asked if she could come sit with Josh and Suzanne and Ryan let her go. The children talked and Melanie and Suzanne chatted too.

"I think it went well," Melanie assured her.

"I hope you're right. I think Tiffany would ruin Beth's life if the judge ruled in her favor."

When the judge returned to his chair, Tiffany's lawyer gave his summation, reinforcing Tiffany's pain and her desire for a child, skipping over the fact that she couldn't have a child because she had chosen sterilization. When it was Mac's turn, he gave an orderly recitation of the facts. Then he described the loving family situation Beth was now in. Finally, he pointed out that Tiffany had ignored Beth until she needed a child to please her wealthy husband. "The lives of children should not be determined by an adult's whimsy," he concluded.

Ryan had prepared Suzanne for the delay while the judge made his decision. However, the judge didn't take any time. He rapped his gavel and said, "I've made my decision."

"I protest, Your Honor," Tiffany's lawyer objected.

"Protest all you want. This is a clear case, and my decision wouldn't change if I waited an hour, a day or a month. In this particular case, the birth mother has evidenced no concern for the child, only for her own needs. It would be a travesty of justice to allow her to ruin this child's life just because she gave birth to her. I rule in favor of Ryan Walker and his family. Beth stays with her family.''

The courtroom cheered as everyone congratulated Ryan and Suzanne. The judge rapped his gavel. ''Bring yourselves to order.'' When everyone grew quiet, he said, ''Dismissed'' and rapped again.

Ryan reached over the rail and lifted Beth into his arms, hugging her close.

''Is somepin' wrong, Daddy?'' she asked.

''No, Beth, everything's great. The judge said you get to come home with me and Susie and Josh.''

''And Mandy? They won't take her away 'cause I broke her arm?'' Beth asked anxiously.

Suzanne patted her arm. ''No, honey. That was an accident. Everyone knows you didn't mean to hurt her.''

''But no more pushing someone who's younger than you.''

''Yes, Daddy.'' She hugged his neck. ''Does that mean we can have an ice cream on the way home?''

Ryan exchanged a look with Suzanne. Then he agreed to the ice cream.

EVEN THOUGH Beth had tried to save some of her ice cream for Mandy and had gotten it all over herself and the back seat, the Walkers were in a happy mood. They were supposed to meet their friends at The Last Roundup for a celebration dinner.

Suzanne was in charge of washing the dress and Beth, while Ryan and Josh handled the truck. Mandy, of course, complained about not getting ice cream, but Ryan promised her ice cream for dessert at the restaurant.

Suzanne found a quiet moment while the children napped to think about the events of the day and the future. She wasn't sure how Ryan would react. She knew as long as he'd needed her to save Beth, he'd pretended to love her. But he'd never once mentioned the word *love*. Could she continue allowing him the use of her person because he liked sex, when he didn't love her?

She was sitting in the kitchen with the light off. It was a cloudy day. She saw movement on the porch and stared in surprise as Tiffany opened the door and came into the kitchen.

Tiffany looked furtively around and crept through the kitchen, not seeing Suzanne. Suzanne silently got up and called Cal Baxter at once and told him in a whisper what Tiffany was doing. Then she called the barn. Ryan answered the phone and she told him to come at once.

When she heard Beth scream, she hurried to the girls' room. "What are you doing?" she demanded.

Tiffany looked up. "I'm taking my baby and you're not going to stop me."

"Oh, really? You think you can threaten me and that will make me let you walk out with Beth?"

Suzanne was stunned when Tiffany drew a gun out of her purse. "Yes, I do. Don't you agree?"

"No. Even if you shoot me, I'll still fight for Beth."

Tiffany gave her a vicious smile. "Oh, I won't

shoot *you*. I'll shoot the other kid. And I'll tell the judge it was an accident. He'll believe me.''

With her eyes on Tiffany, Suzanne said, ''Mandy, go to Josh, quickly.''

Mandy had not understood the conversation, but she did as she was told. Tiffany stared at Suzanne, even going so far as to raise the pistol, but Suzanne moved to block her line of fire.

''Turn Beth loose and get off our property.''

''Your property? So you married him for what you'd get? Believe me, it's not worth it.''

''Suzanne?'' Ryan called as he reached the back door. Tiffany was startled, and fear came into her eyes.

''I also called the sheriff. He'll be here soon.''

''You bitch! How dare you!''

''That's not a nice word,'' Beth pointed out. ''Daddy told me so.''

Ryan burst into the room. ''What the hell!'' he exclaimed when he saw the gun.

''I'm taking my child. And if you try to stop me, I'll shoot her,'' Tiffany said, pointing to Suzanne.

Suzanne was shocked when Ryan agreed to let Beth go.

''Ryan! No!''

''It's okay, Susie. Her plan won't work.''

''Yes, it will.'' Tiffany yanked on Beth's arm.

''Daddy!'' Beth cried.

''Steady, Beth. Do you remember what I told you you should never, never do?''

Beth gave him a curious look. ''Yes.''

''I want you to do it now. She's a mean woman.''

Beth stared at her father. Tiffany looked from him to the child and back again. That was when Beth did as her father had told her not to. She leaned down and bit the hand on her arm. Tiffany screamed and Ryan leaped. Suzanne got Beth out of the way, telling her to go play with Josh and Mandy. Ryan, by that time, had the gun in his hand.

"That was unfair!" Tiffany protested. "I may be infected."

"I don't think stealing my child at gunpoint is fair, either."

"Anyone home?" Cal called from the kitchen.

"Come on, let's go reintroduce you to the sheriff," Ryan suggested, waving for her to go first. As he passed Suzanne, he looped his other arm around her and followed Tiffany.

It didn't take long to explain the situation to Cal. He took the gun and asked for Tiffany's permit. She didn't have one, of course. He arrested her for attempted kidnapping, having an unlicensed firearm and resisting arrest—Tiffany had slapped him before he got the cuffs on her.

"Gee, I hope your lawyer is still close by. You're going to need him." Cal warned her with a grin.

She refused to speak to him, which suited everyone there. He shoved her ahead of him to put her in the back of the patrol car. "We'll see you guys tonight."

Ryan enfolded Suzanne in an embrace, whispering thank-yous into her ear.

"You saved me," she said and pushed out of his arms.

He gave her a funny look, but he went to visit with the children, in case they were still frightened.

DINNER SEEMED LOVELY that night, but Suzanne didn't feel well. She supposed her stomach still had jitters after Tiffany's threat. After eating a little, she began to feel very queasy. She excused herself and went to the ladies' room, where she promptly deposited everything she'd eaten into the toilet.

Samantha came in just as she finished. "Suzanne? Are you all right?"

"Um, yes. I'm just a little queasy. I think it happens every time I'm threatened with a gun."

"Then you mustn't let it happen often," Samantha said with a smile. She reached out and felt Suzanne's forehead. "You don't appear to have any fever."

"No, of course not. And I feel much better than I did."

"Oh, good." Samantha hesitated and then asked, "You wouldn't happen to be pregnant, would you?"

Suzanne turned pale. "What? No! Of course not!"

"How do you know? Do you use protection?"

"M-most times. Not the first time, but it's only been a week or two."

"Well, I asked because it sounds just like pregnancy strikes me. Some women never get nauseated. I feel queasy at once."

The door opened and Jessica and Alex came in. "Is everything all right?" Jessica asked.

"Suzanne lost her dinner."

"I'm sure I'm not pregnant!" Suzanne repeated. The other three women looked at each other.

"I couldn't be. Ryan doesn't want any more children!" and she burst into tears.

Melanie came in. "What's wrong."

"Go tell Ryan to come here," Alex said.

Melanie didn't ask any questions. When she'd gone, Samantha asked, "What are you going to say to him?"

"I'm going to tell him that I'll be representing Suzanne in the divorce and he's going to pay a lot of money and lose all three of his children if I have anything to say about it!" Alex snapped and stepped outside the rest room to wait for Ryan.

Suzanne protested, but the other women promised Alex wouldn't be that mean.

Ryan asked Melanie several questions, but she didn't answer any of them. When he got to the rest-room door, he found Alex standing there with her arms crossed.

"Alex, what's wrong?"

"Do you love Suzanne?"

"Of course I do!" he exclaimed, wondering what was going on.

"Have you told her?"

"I've showed her."

"You idiot, that's sex. Have you *told* her you love her?"

Ryan scratched the back of his neck, trying to think. But it was difficult when he was worried about Suzanne. "I don't know. But I will."

"Did you tell her you didn't want any more children?"

"I—I said something about that. I meant while we were fighting for Beth. What is going on?" he demanded.

"She's in there crying after losing her supper, afraid she's pregnant with a child you don't want."

"Dear God," he muttered and shoved open the rest-room door. "Out!" he roared at the women, grabbing hold of Suzanne when she tried to leave.

When the door closed, he lifted her chin so she was forced to look at him. "When I said no more children, I meant while we were trying to get custody of Beth. I wasn't sure I'd survive losing her. It didn't seem like a good time for planning another baby. But, honey, I love you. I thought you knew that. I've been holding you and loving you every night."

"That's sex!" Suzanne protested, tears again coming down her face.

"No, that's love. I couldn't live without you. I need you more than life itself, sweetheart. If you want a dozen babies, that's fine with me."

"But you said—"

"I didn't mean that. I just meant that I had too much to handle right then. I promise."

She buried her head in his chest and said nothing.

"Are you pregnant?"

She shrugged her shoulders.

"Sweetheart, are you unhappy about being pregnant? I'll help you all I can. Tiffany made it sound terrible, but I'd help you through it. We'll hire a housekeeper and—''

Suzanne looked at him. "*I'm* not unhappy about it if you aren't.''

"Of course I'm not!''

"I don't know for sure. Samantha said to come see her in the morning.''

"Okay. But no more tears, okay? And I'll tell you every day I love you.''

"Good.''

They started out of the rest room. He had his arm around her. "There's just one thing. If this baby isn't a boy, I don't know how I'll face Josh.''

Suzanne gave a wet chuckle. "You'll manage. You always do.''

"I know, but I promised him and I can't go back on my word." With a mock sigh and a kiss he added, "I guess we'll just have to keep trying.''

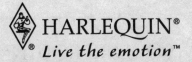

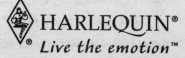